Snow in July

David John Loxton
&
Clió Loxton

Dedication

This book is dedicated to:
Anna, Clió and my son Chiron.

"*ab imo Pectore*"

Limited First Edition (2016)
© David John Loxton 2016

Other books by author
Poetry: *"First Frost"*

Published by

David John Loxton
52 Benedict St, Glastonbury
Somerset, England BA6 9EY.
Tel: 07729 098925

ISBN: 978-0-9955711-1-2

Acknowledgements

I am aware of having accumulated more debts of gratitude than I ever have before on a single book. I am genuinely grateful to all the people who have helped me. Not all of them will be mentioned in what follows.

First, I must thank my printer, Murray Wallace, without whom this book would have remained as a pile of box-files gathering dust somewhere in my home, forgotten to the world. His help and guidance was steadfast even when I must have been an unwanted thorn in his side.

I am grateful to Miranda, whose patience and expertise enabled her to record my work on a computer thing from my long-hand submissions. No complaints there, yet.

I am grateful to my daughter, Clió, who at least gave me the title of the book that was based on one of her own beautiful compositions. I think we bounced off of one another and never gave up even when I thought perhaps it was just another one of my mindless enterprises.

I must thank my Swedish Anna for her companionship through the earlier part of this book. She is unaware that it's published as she was barred from entering this country three years ago. I am not too sure if she'll make it back to feed me crazy foods like beetroot, marmalade and raw potatoes. It sounded odd to me also but I am still here!

I am thankful for my computer technical advisor, Doug, who insisted and virtually made demands that I should go on Kindle (my daughter said it was a dating website that caused some concerns for a moment).

I am super grateful to anyone who buys a copy - The Taxman's knocking on the door..... and I can't hide under the stairs anymore. It's full of books.

Short Stories

Have you ever thought of Woodlouse Farming
or dying and being
reincarnated as a Tree?

Ever thought of really keeping a Promise or feeling deeply for the
welfare of worms?

Well —, it's all in this book together with a splash of the most
incredible true stories that I've ever dared to pen. Hearsay always
leads to imagination and to be creative fends off the Madness!

Poetry

People like my poetry - it's real. In order to express emotions you
have to feel it. Not in the mind. Not in the Heart but from the Spine.
The very backbone that drags us through our life experiences.

D.J. Loxton 2016

Index to Contents

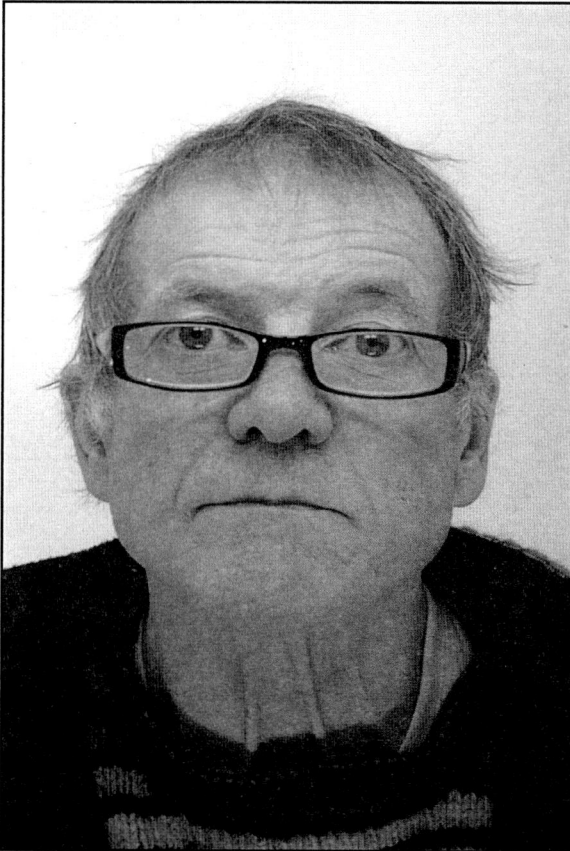

David John Loxton

David John Loxton was born in Shapwick, Somerset in 1955 and grew up in the countryside. He spent a big part of his life as a school teacher until his resignation in 2005. Today he lives on a modest pension and supplements his life-style by being self-employed but to be honest, not wanting the work. He just wants to read and write and feed his House-sparrows with stale bread.

A Book of Snippets

Foreword
Having a new addition to the family has many pleasures but, also, the uncertainty of real purposeful parenthood, holds hidden worries. These uncertainties are liable to ruin the chances that you have to be loving, responsible parents; but heed my thoughts - I am no role model.

The Conception
I remember well, playing a big part in the conception of my two children. I remember the warmth and comfort for my partner - I even remember the hangover the following morning. I even remember the bed spinning, I wanted to get off. The empty bottles spilling out onto my neighbour's right-of-way. The cat looking up to me, as if I had shit in the kitchen and would blame her.

I was stunned when she told me the good news, but, above all the feelings, I felt somewhat amazed to know that after a lifetime of disbelief, something was happening that would change my life forever. I even thought that, maybe in years to come, I'd have a new drinking partner, and he or she would have enough money to fund my habit. We can all dream. Men are also allowed to speculate the impossible.

Romance
Easy. First you feel sorry for someone, then you invite her out to dinner (regardless of the cost, steak suppers and wealth usually clinch the final deal of 'Sex at Midnight'). The Romance worked well for the first few weeks, and, with reluctance, I endured the next mind-bending five years that nearly put me in a mental hospital.

Three weeks of fun, and then a lifetime of calling 'Mercy'. She always looks better than me, but at least I am honest and do not require to baste myself like a turkey at the Last Supper. Never felt like eating at midday, too much time avoiding the overspill on the rim of a glass.

She could talk endlessly about the most boring subjects on earth, but, more remarkable, was that her mother, step mother, and close family members could all compete against each other with one main aim - who could bore me rigid first. This, I felt, was somewhat like a competition, similar to the ones we created at Christmas. Those 'family bonding' games that always ended in tears. I made excuses and carried out important tasks, like chopping firewood, or having to spend the day fixing that urgent job in the workshop. I got so good at it that I wished I'd been paid an hourly rate.

I looked forward at the day's end; to see them leave, wave them off, wave goodbye to her step-mum's shell suit that was lowering the tone of the neighbourhood. I found it increasingly hard to fathom out how the father had married her. Maybe he was too pissed to notice at the time before it was too late, and the gold rings had been exchanged; or maybe it was just bad luck, and she was the only raffle prize remaining. Surely, when you skittle-for-a-pig you're meant to eat it anyway?

I wondered if they had been educated further than house-training? I was right in one thing, which was to keep away from any girl from beyond the bridge that joins the South West from the others, the ones that brag about 'new books' that, to me, are history.

"I am reading a book on obsessional disorders", they'd say, and I'd believe them because they only choose books with big, glossy covers and lots of pictures. After repeatedly banging my head on the wall, avoiding the cracks in the backyard and constantly washing my clean hands, I would agree that maybe there is some degree of truth in it, but there's usually an underlying cause, and mine is that they're getting on my tits.

There are many early warning signs to heed caution when you, finally, are invited back for the traditional night cap of coffee after a long evening of pretending that you're genuinely interested in her corn-dolly collection and how they relate to the pagan earth-goddess.

The first warning is the Ikea everything. Strictly no taste, nothing original. The biggest warning is her music collection; keep clear if it's mainly ABBA, make excuses, and go whilst there is still no hope or you'll end up humming them in your head forever; this type of music being a rare form of cultural brainwashing.

One excellent method of getting rid of visiting relatives, is to keep changing your accent and create an imaginary friend. Tell them there's a nasty virus about that damages brain cells, and you won't see them for dust. Isn't it amazing how people remember to leave early as they've forgotten to feed the cat?

Make the most of this romantic event. Light candles and pretend it makes the room ambient. Don't tell the truth - that the electricity meter ran out yesterday. In times like these, a small blowtorch always comes in handy for reheating the pre-prepared ready meals. The blowtorch works convincingly. You saw a similar demonstration on 'Master Chef'. Not only that, but it also plays a big part in taking the chill off the room.

The main differences of her parents are your bank balances. You have little or no money or savings. When money comes to you it's quickly swallowed up in some outstanding debts.

They have money, and they are going to keep it. The greedy, selfish bastards. They like to see others struggle. It gives them something to talk about other than the golf club, or their Frank Sinatra memorabilia that I will struggle to take to the charity shop when they've snuffed it to the Great Fairway in the Sky.

To be polite, you'll say your home in minimalist, which basically states quite clearly that you haven't anything. They, on the other hand, have a modern three-bedroom with a shag-pile throughout, covered by the biggest pile of crap that you'd ever seen.

Your neighbourhood is bounded by fields that your children, and the pets, like to play in. Their boundary is a training ground for terrorists. Your local paper shows off some old codger's prize marrow, theirs feature stabbings and murder weapons, blurred CCTV images of people robbing shops, with headlines saying 'Have you seen this man?' 'No we have not.' 'He doesn't live near us.'

Their neighbourhood is surrounded by the constant, uninterrupted sound of traffic moving 24-7. Your nights are only disturbed if a mouse farts in the outhouse.

The carefully planned tea-time, with its banquet-styled array of coloured food, is always enough to send my small children into overdrive.

"What boundless energy they have," says Mrs Ignorant. "Yes, I am sure that if you pick them up and shake them, they'd rattle. Don't, whatever you do, light the blue touch paper that's sticking out their backsides."

The sink top, the draining board, displays an orderly row of the many empty tins of the food that she'd considered and chosen from the corner store in her quest to poison the world. How considerate, right down to the sweaty ham sandwiches she'd painstakingly made, even in a time when we were vegetarian. She never spared a thought for us. Correct, she'd never spared a thought.

The Step-Mother brags of always being a housewife, meaning to me that she's alone most of the time, and fully absorbed in every soap-opera on the TV! She plans her life according to the TV Times, and is really disappointed if a programme suddenly has to change for important news coverage of a war in some part of the world.

The father talks of his time in industry, making meaningless products for three-bedroom home builders. He talks of his middle-management roll, having started at the age of five on the shop floor and working his way up. His long service award is framed, and takes pride of place next to the Mickey Mouse wind chimes.

We feel sorry for them and reach for the tissues. They think we're oversensitive. We think that they think that also.

No-one is allowed to speak when 'EastEnders' is on. One may only be prepared to give out a low sigh when a life-threatening heart attack has taken full effect. When the final credits roll up the widescreen TV, to the discerning invalid, they may resemble an obituary.

Holidays, oh, how we love them. Two weeks under damp canvas, wearing damp clothes. Eating tinned foods and the slimy bacon always available at campsite shops. The bacon never fries, it sort of poaches itself amid the injected water and preservatives. The make-shift clothes line. The make-shift everything. When the worlds collide, and the great bomb falls, at least we have troubled ourselves in the fine art of survival. I've had times when we were so skint and hungry that I often wondered about eating other campers.

"What happened to the family in the red tent?"

"They moved on last night to a better place." Heaven can wait... "Pass me that tender bone."

The parents go to the same place every year. A mobile home like a city housing estate of portable buildings, better known to those more educated minds as a caravan park.

A view from your window of the window and the occupants of the adjacent tin shack. A posh tin shack with the options of a hook-up too low to the ground to warrant injury, should you decide to hang yourself and remove the misery. The buildings are so close, like defunct railway carriages, they form endless lines of rusting metal slowly eroding away and devaluing daily. The parents know the neighbours on first name terms, maybe even sharing a barbeque and stories of their years in industry. Each day they arise early, go through scheduled routines, and retire to bed at the same time. So passes the glory of the world.

After Dinner With Mints

I know when you'd had dinner......
To know you well is - ,
To share the credit card - ,
When no favours were left in a bank.
No disgrace now for whatever
Just a laugh as you realised - ,
He was no better than me.
I knew you well,
In your short dress.
Amid the general public that showed concern,
For your aging knees,
A bit like cabbages, green and knobbly,
full of breaking out, but confined
To the garden where in your humdrum ways
You planted that very crop,
To make me turn away from my learnings.
I knew you so well - ,
As the partner who said
She was "Well - bred"
Then turned around on some crazy speedboat
To run me aground
I fail to remember the vegetables (I am vain). Even the garnish that
you'd always given me.
I turned around to listen to my thoughts,
Then put the radio on, maybe the T.V.
Fed up, like a fad of tradition - , when everyone can now go naked.
Or even announce their purity to the unmarked God.

I listened hard to THAT song
Fearing something unreal.

Then turned the volume switch higher
To make me some place else.
Dance alone.
Dance as always trying to be some - ,
Eternal friend
Some kind of easy guy that can sort
All sorrows - ,
But,
The breakfast table continues to wait
For that warm welcome.
Where you can once again stain,
These glasses with your lipstick
And make your own mark on the lipstick
Of my own choice.
To swallow life's meaning
Doesn't make much sense to me.
The Bob Dylan songs stay fixed
Like your father's lock at the dead of night
When I couldn't work a thing
Fumbled in the darkness,
Hoping for my dream.

What is leftover?
Is it in a bag for that puppy
That you make such a fuss of
Or, is it me?
I cannot imagine where you have been
The lovely moments, the sights the scenes
But one bare time in my head after those stints,
"Whatever happened to that coffee - with mints?"

The Disappearance (1960)

Mrs Ings was not at home. The corner shop door was wide open to her covered window displays above the door, waved in silent protest about a change, maybe a change in the weather but who really knows such answers? Mrs Ings was - just to get it right - not there!

The polished pine flooring was clean not even leaving a footprint of any man who dared to help himself to a packet of Woodbine cigarettes from her small glass tobacco display cabinet. The small worn-out fridge in the corner whirled in disbelief with a motor that always hummed a new song, maybe to others and old song with a faint melody of bygone times. Mrs Ings was not at home. She just wasn't there.

The birds of the air settled around her shop. Chirping in words and choruses only known to bird loving people. They danced inside that village shop and helped themselves to her tiring bread display. They even dared to dance upon the counter! Next to an open till filled with coppers and a few hard-earned shillings they did not seem to care a fig about anything today. Today the master was away. Gone. Gone someplace else. a time when even the birds who reside within this olden village could be released into new-found freedom.

Old John the bachelor staggered in. Still clutching an empty hip-flask from his waistcoat pocket. The birds flew out in a quick exit and all John could do was gaze, gaze at the quietness that had overcome this usual busy space. He looked around for service. Rested his old working arm upon the counter and rapped the edge with hammering knuckles. No response. No service, so he troubled himself to cuss the moment, lifted up his worn-out body and removed himself back out into the strong springtime sunlight. The silence settled as softly as the dust that rimmed the bay windows disturbed by John's hands and all and everything became calm again.

Footsteps. Footsteps overbearing outside clip-clopping like a horse as it goes about its journey. Carrying closer up to the open door, the hob-nailed boots stopped and their owner peered within. Stroking the stubble on an unshaven face, a man wearing working clothes furnished with a flat-cap upon his head looked even harder to see if anyone was there to help him on his journey to the moor again to cut the peat field. Nobody was there, so he clip-clopped away to his world of work.

A remote hamlet built on the edge of an even more distant and forgotten wilderness. The Somerset levels stretched out far like a flat open hand to grip the very comfort of the Mendip Hills.

A piece of the beautiful tapestry of a county that was slow to change for almost everybody was unaware of its sacred existence, 1955, a good year for turnips and elderflower champagne. A good year for other harvests. A time when the sweet meadows filled every cottage with pollen. When the only noise created was that of passing tractors and the endless heart-beating thumps of diesel pumps draining the moorland in the distance.

But the question remained unanswered. Where on earth was Mrs Ings? Where was this shopkeeper always standing behind the counter, slowly chewing a small piece of cured ham?

A calamity is rarely witnessed in the village except when someone dies or is injured in their duty to labour hard amongst dangerous farming machinery. A calamity does not exist. It's even a word that remains unspoken because it's too educated for village folk. All vocabulary resides in short staccato sentences that echo the memories of poor schooling and local accents.

My mother came shuffling down the rough cobbled drive still wearing those worn-out slippers with the missing pom-poms that had been removed as useful playthings for the cat.

She stood alone. She stood upright (she wasn't used to standing upright - always bent over the sink in our kitchen).

"Where is Mother Ings? - Where now is she? David! Go now and look in the yard to find her!!"

I was looking innocent. I learnt, in my younger days, never to cross her feelings. Those days of passage where even troubled children still learnt to keep their own ears.

"Going Mother" ..... I said with the very voice of one who knows that maybe he'd lose the ears that he was born with.

That yard was open and smelt of paraffin. The stench always settled me down into thinking that some of the poorer people didn't have a log or a coal fire. "They must be worse off than us." I'd say as I made a journey across an open yard that made the surface of the corner pond a rainbow of interesting colours.

In a quiet corner was a body. Not moving but still, - in a quiet corner. The sunlight gazed down upon me and I, in thought, made a hasty exit to shoulder myself against the grey unsettling walls. It was Mrs Ings!! - in all her glory!!

My childhood senses told me that she was very much alive, she moved.

"Look here now, David. Look what I've found." She seemed to settle down by an old log that knew no better to help than my Sunday-School Scriptures.

"Primroses!" she exclaimed "Look how beautiful they are." She mused and said - "I always liked the colour yellow"...

The Promise

Father promised that he would take us out in the car, but he couldn't - it was broken. 'Something about a distributor', I heard him say with his clearly spoken voice. A powerful voice ready to captivate any audience. This time he was talking directly to our mother, but just to overcome his disappointment, he uttered out that statement as if he was on a stage. Yes, Father had promised to take us to town. He promised to mend the broken gate, the wonky window, and a thousand other things. A master of giving out promises, and a better master of not being capable of keeping them. He was far too busy.

Father promised, on his wedding day, to love and to obey. Mother must have known. She didn't expect either. He promised to regain her diamond ring from the pawnbroker's shop, and in the same sentence, promised he'd buy a better one, maybe a brighter one with a real stone but no, he thought it better to buy his daughter a pony.

She ended up with a bicycle, but she always called it 'Black Beauty'.

My family came from poor stock. Father insisted we were humble and there was money in the bank. He promised to send me to the public school, and I believed him so much that I won the only scholarship. I was a Day Boy at a local school, and the boarders amid the Gothic architecture even reminded me of my humbleness. I 'was' the only Day Boy.

Father promised us all that we'd never go hungry, and when we were big enough to know the difference between a weed and a plant, taught us to use a large array of garden tools. The plants grew and our bellies were full. When Mother said she had a surprise dinner for us, I was equally surprised to notice it was beans-on-toast again. Life was always full of surprises. Father was right again. We never went hungry. When we grew older, Father provided us with books with 'How to do it' titles and, as the years passed, things improved. The wonky window was repaired. The garden gate was fixed, and our lives changed for the better. Yes, Father maintained his promises, and we all became craftsmen to uphold his words.

Father was a writer. Mother said to us, as we warmed ourselves around the fire, that he had a raw talent. We wondered about such suffering, because raw was a word that always hurt us. Yes, Father was a writer. Late evening times, the faint light glimmered in his shed well into the early hours, and we would all fall asleep listening to his spoken words as he recited his raw thoughts. Sometimes we thought he was in pain, but he always appeared cheerful the next morning.

School holidays kept their usual conformity of long awaited sleep-ins.

Father promised us sunshine, but it invariably rained. 'Food for the thirsting flowers' he said, as we played in the muddy puddles, and came to understand that wet days are always better than school days. "One day, I promise you all a grand family outing", he said, and as the years passed, we continued to wait. Watched the clock hands turning the hours. Watched the second hand stick in its restless position as the battery inside ran out of energy.

One day, one of those mornings to be precise, a visitor came to the threshold of our door. He looked important. He wore a suit. A green silk suit that made him sparkle in the sunlight. In his arms he carried a black folder with a large metal bulldog clip that held a silver pen fast.

He talked to my father. Something about an uncle who lived in New Zealand who had spent his life in the mines, who had sadly died of old age. Then he talked to my father about a great sum of money that our uncle had left for us in his will. A vast sum of money! far more than could ever be counted in a lifetime.

Father immediately ordered a new distributor, then caught the bus to the nearby town. We all sat around the kitchen table looking at each other, and wondering about the kind uncle whom Father had never mentioned, even on special occasions when sometimes he'd tell us a secret or two.

Late afternoon, Father returned with his arms laden with over spilling plastic supermarket bags. We were still sitting in the same places, still wondering. He placed a large, crusty loaf of bread on the table, so fresh that the smell from the bakery seemed to have followed it home. He placed a large slab of cheese on the table, followed by some small spring shallots. Reaching up to a higher shelf, he took down the last bottle of elderflower champagne and poured its fizzy contents into a line of glasses.

"Sit here Mother. I've something special for you," said Father, beckoning her to the chair at the head of the table. He handed her a small, pretty box covered in blue velvet, with an equally pretty bow on its top. Mother opened it, and gazed for a long time. Looking up at her was a parcel of glowing light as the sun danced upon the clear cut facets. A diamond ring of the finest quality embraced her heart with the same tenderness as the first one he had given her so many years ago.

That late evening, a Land Rover appeared at the gateway, towing a trailer. The farmer opened the heavy tailboard, and out stepped a dappled pony.

Yes, Father promised us a thousand things, and, true to his words, he made sure that a promise cannot be broken. One thing though for sure, is the unspoken fact that, although he made so many, he honoured his words, and, as for us, well, we always believed truly in one man's undivided love for his family.

A Walk to Street

A clear day in early summer as I walked to town,
Half stumbling with an annoying club-foot.
That constantly wanted a change in my intended direction.
My intentions though, were true,
I had to go forwards to a goal where there was no ball
To kick back to the boys that played on the open field.
Past the forgotten unforgiving factory buildings, the Tannery
Derelict, but somehow filled with romance
To workers who married their sweethearts from its weekly wage
Somehow, I could almost imagine them dancing
Saturday evenings on a lonely club dance floor with perfume
Concealing the daily stench of wet sheepskins
The bridge stands between us
Stonewalled, she embraces life under life's burden of hurry, of
Work or impending disasters.
Upon the bridge, I stood and waited as I always do
For change.
Interrupted in my gaze, a bird flew towards me
Haphazard in its movements, like a drunken man trying to get home.
"Who is this visitor?" I asked myself until he turned away
With furtive thoughts to safeguard himself.
A flash of radiant blue, and he disappeared -
"Kingfisher" I mused at the boy within me.
It made the day complete - why worry
About the car being broken again.

Mrs Jurey's Quiet Discontent

Mrs Jurey sat listening into the quiet hour, when even her own thoughts were written on some form of comfort.

She was wise. She had a crazy sort of composure about her usual habits, which were very Victorian.

She was from the souls of the blessed, everyone that had journeyed to the Sunday-School blessings, that she herself had caused. Her own beliefs and sufferings on all those Sunday mornings.

Mrs Jurey lay quietly in her bed, wrapped up in old blankets and eiderdowns coloured by the smell of her own elderly decay. She was wondering if the night would be okay? She was wondering if the boys would just go home to their beds. She even wondered if they had parents??

Silence is golden until she heard her window rattle with a very uncharacteristic knock. The house itself felt it was being beaten to death.

A loud knock and then another. She, that silent person, drew the covers of a sheet up upon her face fearing an intruder. The clock by her bedside ticked out the moments, and she lay like a corpse hidden in the dark.

There was the distinctive sound of glass sprinkling over the small porch floor. The sound of the tinkles, that she herself felt in her childhood memories when her own father played those silly Christmas tricks of how wonderful moments can be!

A dull thud. An even harder one, and the invader was within her world. Footsteps. Footsteps by an old boot, unfamiliar to her ageing eyes and ears. Plodding relentlessly in the failing light at eventide. All outside gives the very moment, a great time when fear itself becomes locked in the darkness.

She gripped that sheet tightly with arthritic hands, and saw them glow white. Fear is always white. Fear has no boundaries to any common man.

The faint light, always addressed to the common man, gave this new person a chance to even reckon to himself. A chance to even look at himself. The warrant to give him only maybe 15 hours of community service (that's if he had done any wrong).

Marbled pathway through the porch-way, like a dart that follows up to the stairwell and the next divide. So solemn are stairs at midnight, when everybody is free. Mrs Jurey still lies in bed. Still waiting for her freedom, those moments when we all loved her.

Movements on the threshold that leads further up to her sacredness. Higher up to the landing, when the sound on threads feel just like belonging to God (or whatever he represented). Maybe Jacob was still climbing that ladder?

She lay silent and said a small prayer of forgiveness to her lord - something about feeling sorry for herself, when a long time ago, she had been chased from a neighbour's garden for stealing apples. She herself was wondering if God himself, or whatever he represented unto the Holy Faith, had really bothered to listen to her meek story.

"The meek will inherit the earth," she said. "But what about Wednesday when I failed to put my rubbish bin out for the morning collection?"

Life is a story and so is a moment. One of those days when you knew in your heart that the lock on the back door needed a serious look-at - a long time ago - but you, in faint honesty, thought in your heart that it would be okay for a few more years, or maybe when the money was better.

Mrs Jurey is an old lady, and she lives her golden life. No need for the small tin with its rimless mouth, unrelenting, as she, in her beauty, cuts yet another finger to rinse under the cold tap in that faithful kitchen, when even the hot tap is not used for fearing the quarterly bill. Typical of Mrs Jurey, she had not noticed the door slowly opening with its usual squeak, as the ancient hinge pushed up against friction.

"Who's there, who's there?" She said in a soft voice, decrying love itself for labour and love for its portions.

"It's me mother! I heard a message from your neighbours that you hadn't been seen for a while, so I've come to check up on you."

"Now, now John, you should surely know that my spare key is always under the terracotta flower-pot in my outhouse."

My Greatest Adventure

My first glance was to squint and peer through sleepy eyes. Eyes that had been on some form of crazy journey where everything had been cosy, where everything was warm - lost in perpetual darkness. A world where nobody quarrelled or fought. A place where I could cuddle up against the endless pumping sounds of a parent who shared her blood with me.

For a time I shared all that my mother ate, even the odd glass of wine, or the cigarettes that made me turn against her love for me... I was to learn that even parents can be cruel at times. I was prodded many times by an unseen hand that nearly blinded me. I was even given an ultrasound completed by a smooth, cold dressing of jelly.

I had no injury. I hadn't fallen - so why are they checking this fickleness that starts to anger me and makes me kick!

My father often put on loud music. The Celtic drums beat me down into submission. They didn't know that, given a choice, I preferred Jazz (and would be a good double-bass player, but only to the rhythm of sixty beats a minute).

When I came, it was somewhat a rush, liken to floodwater that always caused a scene or two. Those times when parents seem to value the material things that could always be replaced. My father ruined his best shirt that would be a haunting for my days, until he died.

Passed away still moaning of the day when I was born.

Those days when all his wishes were to have a son who would always keep him in debt. What did they give me? LIFE

Joy to the World

On Easter Sunday, she gave me a golden egg. I gave her nothing. I know full well that she expected a bunch of daffodils, stolen from the neighbours' garden when the evening had settled down to sleep and rest. Today she gave me an egg. I got a strange feeling that she was unhappy, and had to whack me on bones that I happen to live in. The bruise showed she cared.

It's a bit dull, but cider is a good painkiller. It breaks off the hassle of the world so much, that I believe that I am part of a cartoon that Walt Disney had forgotten, or never dared to express. Whether on paper or in pubs.

The stamping of feet overhead, and I knew she was still at home. My residence. Watching the ceiling lights also playing a dance to her anger and brute thoughts. Flickering on and off (a small electrical problem) like the first disco when we danced with one another without a care in the world. The staggering of loose feet upon pavements that failed to take me to my own home. Just someplace just as cold as mine. With the cheap coffee that dusted the rims of mugs stained in some other lost purpose with little or no taste.

"Who's calling you now, David?" she said, in that clearly decayed voice that I thought for a while, she could break glass. Ripe for resurrection upon a papal bed, where the nymphs are only spread for special occasions when that prophet could eagerly dare to loosen his flowing gowns.

I went to church. The vicar was naked. He told us we had a problem. I thought the same. Dog collar and roses brought in from the flower girls that he chastised in front of a calendar of some other breed. Font off. I turned to that vicar before I took him to exercise in the graveyard, and watch him so obediently raise a leg to relieve himself on my father's grave. So stollen as bread from my mother's kitchen when we were growing up and believed in religion so much so that at Winter Time, we were blessed with the faint reminder of Church-Coal. A time to feel a little bit colder, wondering what mother had got up to in the Vicarage back at Autumn time then the Walnut Tree showed clearly that everything is green. Unsettled as the dust rising in our coalhouse. Isn't life strange, I was peeling off the remainders of yesterday onto another burnt frying pan.

Easter Time! A triumph, but where are my biscuits? I thought looking down at my dog who in thoughts looked up with crumbs on his face and said 'Thank you'. No dust to taste even. No mark of cinnamon upon my tongue. That dog must like spices - what an interesting animal, I thought, as he left my table guided by a firm boot up his ass.

Why is it, every year, that before the Bank Holiday Monday, we always have to crucify some guy who's been dead for ages. My own father got only one ceremony, and then was forgotten in some small corner that would all be covered in nettles.

No, Jesus has to suffer for us every year, and even the disbelievers - or those who worship other gods - still get the same time off work, but are only too quick to complain if we upset their faiths.

Maybe Easter should be given a new name, like 'Aftermath', or 'Sincerely Yours', or if I refrain I could say it's 'Halloween...'

The Sad Story of Holly Moffit

Little Holly Moffit was a sweet child, she always studied hard at school, and kept her hair clean and tidy. Her dad, he had a troubled background and had believed his life total, fulfilled now with a worthy family until his life was thrown away at his partner's Xmas party...

"Alone again, once more a single dad, even though I had taught so many, so little time to teach my own" - he sighed.

He was very proud of her, and because she was born at Christmastime, she was given her name, Holly.

Holly loved to dance to her favourite songs. Sometimes she sang along to them, bounced around on the bedroom floor. Holly loved feeding her pets, but most of all - Holly loved climbing trees!

She had her dreams. At the top of a huge elm tree in summertime, she could be seen. Her golden hair flying like a flag on the uppermost branches. At the top of the noble and wise oak tree, she could be seen, her hair flying like a flag on its uppermost branches.

"Look at me, Dad!" she would often say. She had climbed so many different trees safely with no help from any grown up. Very old grown up people always said to her father as he read the newspapers in the park:

"Is that your little girl in the tree? ... She might fall, she is very high up!"

Father gave his usual answer, sneering over the brim of his thoughts - yes.

"But, is that your daughter in danger of falling?"

Father gave his usual answer - "Yes, but only if you shout at her. My daughter is a tree-climber!"

With his proud fatherly ways, he would continue to read his paper, including stories of young people that had fallen from trees, office blocks, and windows left open by understanding parents.

Holly did not understand her dad too well. He was always too busy in his workshop, inventing things like everlasting toothpaste, fizzy drinks that made him giddy and crazy ideas of travelling to the stars. Holly know fully why dad never climbed trees - He was always too giddy, and often complained of headaches caused by fizzy drink experiments.

She did not object at all to his experimenting. She has also tried his new blend of dandelion and elderberry fizz, and it made her giddy also.

"One day, one day," she thought, "maybe Dad might invent something useful..." and she went quite silent, laying in bed at night-times, trying to settle down to his constant crashing around downstairs ('more experiments', she thought). Then turned over to beautiful dreams.

At breakfast time Dad was not ready, yet Holly was hungry. She danced into his bedroom, she danced like a grey squirrel, up and around branches of things so sublime but so real to youth, and her imagination... A room festooned by spiders, and knowledge of a lost path. That covering of antiques so old that it made him older than his true age, and his crazy collection of Black Forest Cuckoo clocks that somehow never bothered him, in their constant erratic chiming that never, ever, woke him.

"How old are you, Dad?" Holly said, her young eyes looking up at dark furniture that she was accustomed to.

"I am as old as the hills," he said, turning over like a man slowly beaten to death by hooligans, "but I am not as old as an oak tree - yet."

Holly thought of trees again, and wanted to climb. Holly thought of trees again, and wanted Dad to get up and show her a new one. One new tree, and one new challenge.

So dad sorted himself out with a cold shower, much shouting from the damp bathroom, and followed through somehow with the perfect breakfast (dad's are a bit like that, especially being MY dad).

They journeyed out. They journeyed far. Over and over endless fields troubled by angry farmers waving sticks and shouting absurdities.

"Get off my land!"

Holly said "Are they okay, Dad?" in sweet innocence. And Dad said, as he sat down for a cigarette, troubled by a damp match - "Don't worry about them sweetheart, they only borrow this land for their lifetimes," then puffed a vapour of smoke onto the restless world, stirring flies from the ground that had settled on steaming cow dung. "Who are we, Dad?" she said, as she settled on the dead log that he had given himself to sit on.

"We are Golden, sweetheart! We are the Best! The best of good that could ever happen to my troubled life" - "How could that ever happen, Dad?" You're all alone now, and I'd love to be your little helper."

Dad gave his knowing glance; Dad gave his knowing smile. Touched a young shoulder, Pat on Pat, on back, then smiled... and paused, "I can see a tree from here! - Let's go!!!" His cigarette stub thrown to the correct direction. his knowledge only shown by the glint of a sparkle in his eyes that reminded him of his own childhood, when his own father would beat him with a stick - for climbing trees.

Through the growing fields they walked, gaily skipping over thistles with the warmth of sunshine on their backs.

A great hawk swooped into the bushes with a crash!! and dreamy sparrows stumbled everywhere bewildered, "What was THAT?" they all said together.

"Did you see THAT, DAD!!!?" Remarked an ever increasing youngster.

"Sorry sweetheart, it must be these glasses, they're varifocal!! It's a bit like looking perfectly and then a bit like looking through jam jars! He mused and then Holly mused and at the same time thought: "Maybe the dandelion fizz is not his only problem."

At the bottom of a small valley, where the moles live in their own communities, they saw a Grand Tree! So grand it should have been written in BLOCK CAPITAL LETTERS!! (AND SURE ENOUGH IT WAS).

"What tree is that, Dad?" Said the ever enquiring Holly.

"That, Sweetheart, is a sycamore! It apparently is a weed amongst the hedgerows."

"Well, Dad," she said, laying her frenzied jumper on the five bar gate, her arms draped upon the wood, folding like an envelope that nestled her chin upon her hands. "Well, Dad!! That's the biggest weed I've ever seen - but it looks very much like A TREE!!!"

"Let's hug it first," said Dad, as he stumbled over rocky roots, his glasses flying off his face, disturbing marbled white and yellow brimstone butterflies by the score.

The bark was so dry she could get a grip, and, with a strategic push from strong hands that pumped blood from massive arms, she was up!

"Okay? Puppet?" Said Dad, breathing like a man denied of Breath.

"I am up Dad, and I am going higher." - Then in lightening speed - she was gone.

Dad looked out on his world.

Dad look at the moles complaining, then told them all to 'shut up'. Everything disappeared and once again all became silent.

Little sound, save for the gentle touch of the warm breeze fluttering leaves like tiny wind chimes.

"VICTORY! I am Queen of the trees, and this will be my new Queendom!"

"Well done sweetheart! Come down now, we've tea to prepare for later."

"Can I do the spuds as crazy sculptures again tonight, Dad?" Said a beautiful face peering through the branches above him like a golden harvest moon.

"Sure can!" Said Dad, his arms outstretched, ready to catch the expected leap from the overhead canopy.

The great leap that toppled him over, and they rolled down the bank in a burst of pollen and laughter.

They followed the edge of an ancient hedgerow, hundreds of years old, and on the walk back, Dad said "hello" to all the grazing cows.

"Why do you talk to cows, Dad?" Said Holly.

"Somebody has to," said Dad, and his hand gripped her tiny fingers with a fondness only allowed for loving parents. Holly held tighter also, then swung from his arm that was held out like the branch of the mighty oak (that, apparently, he said he wasn't??)

In a moment of thought next to the hollow pool over-brimmed with green duckweed, the great-crested newts so busy in their card games (CRIBBAGE, WITH LILY PADS AS SCORING BOARDS) turned up to say 'hello' also as they passed.

"What are we doing tonight, Dad? What are we doing tomorrow? What, what is next, Dad?" She sifted through the waist-deep grasses like moving softly through flour, she sifted to raise up hands abundant with golden pollen!

"Look at that, Dad! I am yellow!!"

"You look just like China! Sweetness."

"And where is China?" Said Holly.

"Just on a shelf in the kitchen, surrounded by the ones your mother never took away, or threw at me..."

Tea time was always fun. Lots of preparation of food to the sounds of loud music. It was like an incredible, but edible art lesson. The dessert was especially fun and usually involved. Pastry, but not just - a pastry topping - The two of them together would use different types of pastry, and make three dimensional images of whaling scenes, or dragonflies amongst bulrushes, or whatever came to mind at the time.

The tabby cat affectionately called 'Grub' came in, looked at Dad, then climbed up his body to curl around his neck like a scarf.

Outside, the light was fading, and the bats came out to fly figure-of-eight circuits along the side of the stone cottage, chasing flies and moths.

"look at these, Holly, look at the bats!" said Dad.

Holly looked out and became afraid. "I can see a hand, a big hand!!!"

It took a while for Dad also to see this spectre and explained to the worried child that it was only the house lights shining through the flower pots on the lost boundary wall, casting long finger-like shadows across the field.

The evening was spent sitting by a crackling log-burner, watching 'A Grand Day Out'; the cat flat-out on the carpet, snoring heavily whilst cuddled up to her favourite soft toy of a fish.

Dad dozed, Dad dozed off, his book sliding from his lap to fall with a gentle thud on the floor. Time passed until the fire was reduced to just a series of twinkles in the grate. Dad awoke with a start, a dream had frightened him.

"Holly? Where are you?!"

"I am busy in the kitchen, painting."

"What are you painting, darling?"

"The fridge," said Holly.

On inspection, Dad suggested that maybe he preferred it in white!

The next morning was a day that would change everything. It was a day that would always make Dad feel guilty for the rest of his days.

Even the weather was changing; black, billowing clouds hung heavily in the sky, threatening rain.

"Let's go out on our bikes down the country lanes to the river," said Dad.

"Yeah, yeah, yeah!" whooped Holly, knowing that was an area where the willow trees grew with long winnowed branches that touched down to the waterline.

Down the winding lanes, the verges carpeted in cow parsley overbearing with their pungent smell; down the lanes with wind in their hair, Holly raced forward, her little legs spinning on the pedals due to the low gear she had chosen.

Around the bends, around the blind corners she sped ahead and out of sight, with laughter in the air.

A terrible sound of an oncoming car tyres on soft tarmac. A screech of brakes that failed to stop, and then everything stopped like a pause on a DVD player. Silence sometimes is more expressive than words.

A bike and a small body lay on the road, the front wheel spinning, the only thing that was moving.

The sky suddenly became blacker and even more overcast. A blackbird startled, called out its warning - too late! And then the rain came like tears from heaven.

Then everything faded and went black, as thunder rocked the world.

The weeks passed. The phone calls persisted that Dad was to blame. The mother-in-law said he was evil, the father-in-law said he was a baddie, and the mother said she wished Holly had never stayed.

"Yes," Dad thought, "Yes, blame me."

The weeks went slowly, and Dad went lame and started to use a stick to support his broken body.

The paint eased from doors and windows, but his door remained closed. No more loud music. No more sounds, and the ivy grew to cover his home, save for a small glint of light coming from an inner room. Sometimes, in the dead of night, came a sound of howling like a lone wolf that has lost its litter.

"That is a very tall tree," said Holly, climbing up its ladder-like branches.

"I think it's a Jacob tree - and it's growing above the clouds! I can see dad's house from here."

She had so much energy, and didn't feel at all tired!

Higher and higher to the clouds, then beyond, where she found herself bathed in warmth and white light.

She climbed on, and at the very top, found a city made of gold and precious stones, the sound of jazzy trumpets, but most of all - a forest of 'easy-to-climb' trees (clearly marked by easy-to-read signs)!

"I think Dad should like it here - it's full of jazz musicians!" exclaimed Holly. "There's Nat King Cole singing 'Purple Heaven' - I'm sure Dad once told me that he was dead. Sometimes Dad gets things - SERIOUSLY WRONG!"

"Hello Holly - you're early. We haven't been expecting you for a number of years," said the man with a halo above his head, dressed in fine white clothes, and - with wings?

"Wings?" said Holly "Are you going to a party?

"No, no," laughed the man, "I am a saint!"

"My dad told me not to talk to strangers - even the winged variety!" said Holly.

"But I am the safe variety!" said the saint.

"My dad told me STRAIGHT! No strangers, no sweets in cars, and maybe - NO WINGS!"

"But, I know your dad - he lives on the corner with a cat called Grub. He makes fizzy drinks, drives a Morris Minor with a wing mirror missing because he used it as his extending clothes line. He's a great teacher in the Big school, and, furthermore, he's got one hell of a collection of cuckoo clocks!!!"

"How do you know that then?" said Holly.

"Because, he taught me. He's taught so many of us up here that they call him 'The Main Man'!

"I heard that once," said Holly, "but if he is the 'Main Man', why do his drains still get blocked?"

"That's not his problem at all," said the saint. "It's the neighbours', and, as usual, he gets the blame."

"My dad often is blamed..." said Holly, "but, just to make sure - when's his birthday?"

"Ninth May" said the saint.

"And what's his first name?" remarked Holly.

"David" said the saint.

"And what does David mean?" said Holly.

"It means 'very much loved'" said the saint.

"Then," said Holly, "Why didn't my mum love him for always?"

"I think he might have a drink problem," said the saint.

"Correct!" said Holly, "But, that thing above your head - why doesn't your hair catch fire?"

"Eco-friendly halos with low-energy bulbs - it's all Health and

Safety these days - even in Heaven," said the saint.

"My dad talked of Heaven once," said Holly, "he always said it when he'd been working hard, and didn't get paid a lot of money. He would say that his rewards would be in Heaven. Do you lot up here realise that he could do with a bit of that now?" said Holly.

"Your dad will get his rewards. We have booked him here in the best hotel, but only when his time comes!" said the saint.

"Well, it's about time you lot up here started caring more for everyone, and, not everyone likes jazz music! What's wrong with ABBA, or Dido, or, 'THE KILLERS'!!!"

"I'll forward your complaint to the management, and promise to upgrade our jukebox," said the saint. "Now for the important part. Apparently, you have a glowing school report, good at cookery, and are an expert Tree-Climber. To go back to the Earth, you can be most things, judging by the criteria we have received. May I suggest a doctor, a vet, or maybe a mother's help?"

"Can I go back as ANYTHING?!" said Holly.

"We can endeavour to give you a suitable placement," said the saint.

"Okay," said Holly, "Can I be a TREE?"

And it came to pass, that the jukebox was upgraded, and a contract of life was set up for the young Holly. Her last audience was with the supreme being, who said that he knew of a soul-less olden oak, standing alone in open fields, that she could be reborn in to give it new life and vigour!

The great day came when all the saints gathered around her to give a final blessing. One got too close and his halo burst into fire!

"Low-energy bulbs, huh!" said Holly, as her transparent body floated out of the city walls, and drifted down to the troubled oak that had lost its soul.

The Green Man looked up to the sky, praying for the nectar of rain, then saw Holly descending in a cloud, and said openly - "Thank God for that!" then disappeared into the greenery.

"What happened to Dad?" said Holly, "why, only yesterday, we were going out on our bikes to the river. Maybe I went home to Mum, but I don't remember much after a 'BIG BANG'!"

Her soul soaked into the branches, which gave a beautiful gasp at rebirth, and the grass beneath the trunk shouted 'Reprieve'!

Dad sat in his corner of a room that missed everything, but Dad did his usual things - like eat - with a tired fumble; close the freezer, close the doors, and microwave a moment . Eat up.

And return to sleep, or maybe - that incredible book that he always looked into for direction.

"No direction home," said Dad. "No chance of resurrection - it's my time to fail to see my journey home," and then he was gone.

'Gone on' the woodlice said, 'but, not dead YET!'

The brandy bottle did its usual trick. It rolled upon the worktop, oozing in short, gulping breaths of a time when it was only shared at Christmas...

In his dreams he remembered it all - the parcels covered in wrapping paper so well done that young Holly always fell asleep, too tired by the packaging - too tired to even look at the room festooned in all colours of party blooms.

"I like it here, I quite like this moment," said Dad, the lonely candle burning like a soul lost in the night.

That lonely candle, burning and dripping out his love of Holly and life. .. The bats outside gave a sigh...

That fateful knock on panelled wood that even disturbed the beetles.

"Knock, knock," with its fateful wrap.

"Good morning, sir, we're here to reallocate you to your new home," said a young girl with a boulder of a henchman behind her.

"Do I have to go - now?" said Dad.

"Yes, you have been sectioned under Class 2b of the 1999 Mental Health Act!"

"Don't do Acts," said Dad, "but maybe - have you read that book also?" He tired, and took up his life as a message in a bottle, brimmed only with his thoughts (and sailing ships that he could also see in the distant harbour).

Took up his own hourglass, hugged the suitcase of his life, and watched the small particles of sand in the glass slipping through his tired life...

New beginnings.

A small, one-bedroom flat in a squat of others. a landing that smells of damp pee, and noises at midnight when Dad only wanted his own dreams - NOT THEIRS!

"Where are you sweetheart?!" He called into the night, and then he slipped away again in sleep...

His apartment had a good outlook. A large window peered out onto a beautiful meadow, and in the middle of that vast expanse of openness stood a huge oak tree.

"Think I'll venture out to see that tree, it reminds me of much happier times," said dad. He picked up his stick, pushed a small hip-flask into his coat pocket, then walked out into bright sunlight, his eyes smarting from the glare.

Through the glowing field he walked, the pollen bursting around his body.

"Look at me Dad! I am up here!!" said young Holly - her golden hair flying like a flag in the uppermost branches. Her branches waving like frenzied, excited fingers.

Dad settled himself at the base of the trunk, beneath exposed roots that resembled a chair, and between those roots, he rested his arms to lay his head on the base, his eyes looking up at the beautiful canopy of leaves that offered shelter from the scorching heat.

Looking up, he half believed he could almost see Holly's face above him in that crazy configuration of leaves.

"This is a familiar space," said Dad, "it reminds me of plenty."

He snoozed. He snoozed. He snoozed.

No wind in his face. No time to think bar for the slight twitching of toes in Jesus sandals:

And, all became calm.

The moles looked up from earthen burrows, and all and each one lit candles for the soul of the man re-possessed.

Each day, Dad got stronger in himself, and even tidied his flat (in his own way).

Each day, he learnt to pray for forgiveness, and each day he walked to settle next to his favourite space, a tree, that became his second home.

When the light was fading, he would walk, and he learnt to throw away his stick, and walk again unaided.

When tiredness creeps upon all men, and the moon leaves her body to light the fields in second light, Dad would lie down with his slumbers.

And Holly, well, she would unearth her roots and give him a warm and loving embrace...

And so passes the Glory of the World.

The Trials of Life

Father Green sat in a small receptacle of life. Looked upon his thoughts. So pure as the laundry that was always clean. Looked at the vision of 'The Holy Mary' cast, with worn out cobwebs into his world, of never being complete.

Nothing is pure. Nothing is good, and Father Green continued to ponder on his thoughts.

A life where nothing is open. A faint reminder of his schooling, where his own father had sent him away to the public school, and boarding. A time when in infancy, he needed them most.

Green turned up the covers of the pages he had written. Gazed at their loveliness as if he had been especially chosen to deliver them to a mad congregation. An audience of lay-workers who knew no better than to sit on those ancient pews, and just stare at the high vaulted ceiling.

The seeds of despair often drift across the tables of the wise. A place where even candlelight plays hard with its shadows against the sons of the righteous.

"One small moment of light," said Father Green. "Give me at least a portion of love so that I, too, can send his nectar down."

The dream was gone. Just like the others, when there was no dad or mother to push the swing in the lonely park. To even light up his own troubled lifestyle.

On Saturday, Father Green made his usual attempt to visit the Abbey. So golden once , its disrepair made him think more clearly, like any tramp you find in the eternal gutter. Gave a blessing enclosed by the very shadows of his own disbelief in God being a friend he'd never owned.

"Who is this God?" said Father Green. "What is this spiritual matter that seems to be lost in other adventures?"

He mused. All wise men muse. The likeness of the world

overshadowed him into thinking that he was wrong.

"What is wrong?" said the Reverend Green. That was a small time when God himself made a troublesome journey to speak to such a weak man who had lost his own religion, and a God who had lost a son.

"Belief is another world," thought Green, as he laid small cards upon a table. The chips were down, and Green, in a small entity of Nature, played so badly.

Maybe a little snippet moved across his lap. Fell unto the vacant floor to rest amongst the others from some other morning. Maybe he felt his heart's desire to catch one! Ripe fish he could net them up onto his nicely polished table. The one that always stood firm in its wood, with the sold silver candlestick that his own mother provided for him in her last written testament to the living. When the moment had arrived, and she sadly passed away, with little left behind bar from a stain on the Wilton carpet where her body was found.

The Carnival

Chapter 1

The moon sat high in the western sky. Wise, ripe, and portly, like an ageing cheese that had been hidden away for the right moment. Better still, like a golden coin, shining for the grabbing hands of seamen in their quest for riches overflowing.

The 'Carnival' lay still - less on the quiet ocean, almost silent save for the lap-lapping of small rippling waves against her stout wooden hull, covered in a casing of small barnacles, wet and glistening as precious stones. She was a good, fine ship. A three-master, clung in the draperies of greying sail-cloth festooned by the many riggings, she portrayed the perfect picture of a dark silhouette, against a cloudless sky, in a cloudless night.

Better still, was her beauty in the daytime. Brightly decorated with a mermaid, carved from good timber to make a figurehead.

Fairer than the fairest girls left behind in many a busy harbour or lonesome bay, where the rattling anchor would be released to lay upon the shallow seabed.

Above that clinker-built hull lay the best teak decking, and on that very deck also stood an upright shadow of a man in a tricorn hat with a wooden leg, and under the brim of that darkened hat was an old brow, wrinkled from age, blistered by the raging weather, burning salt sea, and under that brow was a knowing face with beautiful, piercing blue eyes - bluer than even a tropical lagoon, and, underneath the face was a long, dark black tapering trail - of a very long beard. This was no ordinary man - for this was the master of every ocean he surveyed. This was Captain Peg!

He was always standing in the same spot, almost lifeless, with one eye peering out from a brass and leather telescope, and the other on his crew of wild men wilder than lion or tiger, untamed but containing loyal beauty to their leader.

There was Spider, the ship's tailor - and also known as the Master of the Nets. So fast was he at repairing with his needles, that many believed that he had eight arms!!! Relentlessly spinning under deck until long time before the tallow candle had flickered her last breath to leave him alone in the darkness.

There was Saviour, the first mate, and the only one on board who could swim. He was born with webbed hands and feet, and in the terrible storms - should a man be washed overboard - he was the first one to drop everything that he was doing and dive in. He was the only one. Many men he'd saved.

And then there was Norman the Sawdoctor and ship's dentist. The tooth puller who had learnt to write in runic, having found strange writing on small stones on a distant shore in Norway.

Together, Captain Peg and his steadfast crew had sailed around the four continents that stick up and cover sweet Mother Earth. Together, regardless of any real purpose, they had journeyed the four main Compass Points that, even today, give all adventurers the opportunity to travel.

Who needs to aeroplane? Who needs a chartered liner on an ocean cruise? Who needs to worry about the cost, and having to go WITH THE PARENTS?! When, if you are lucky, you may find, one night, that there's a knock-on-the-door, and Captain Peg is looking for some new crew members to help him on his next great mission!!

Chapter 2

For three hundred years, the 'Carnival' had sailed the tumbling waters of life. For three hundred years, the ship had maintained her fixed course, and for three hundred years, Captain Peg's crew had never really complained. They believed him and his crazy decisions.

The great Ocean of Life never offers possibilities, sometimes we have to go with the flow. Go with the surging tidal currents that are capable of forcing the tiller from even the strongest hands. The foaming mouth of so many mad ideas that only young people know, the idea that comes along in your head only to be stamped on by a grown up, leaves little prospects for true creativity.

"Harness the madness that makes your head spin, then we harvest your thoughts together," said Peg.

"There is trouble down under in the hold," the first mate, Saviour, said.

"Trouble!" said Captain Peg "What's the problem?!!!"

"It's starting to wear them out, they're even complaining that the pigs are hungry."

"Go down into the darkest point then, and shovel them up in a bucket of weevils!"

"Weevils, sir?" said Saviour.

"Yes, weevils - alive, alive, O!"

And sure enough, the pigs settled down to grunt contentedly on a wonderful supper.

Scratching under his hat with a small finger, Captain Peg paused to think. He thought - for what might be to many of us - a long, long time.

Suddenly an idea sprung to mind! "Tell Norman to go to my cabin and bring my favourite Map - Chest! The one that's covered in ribbons and bows, gilded by the greatest London goldsmiths. The one with - the mark of a cross on...!!!!"

Captain Peg stood and waited. In the distance under deck could be heard shuffling and banging. The thuds of a heavy load coming closer, thump-thumping up the wooden threads of a well-worn stair into the light of what may appear to many as a beautiful day.

With a final thud the huge casket landed at a safe distance from his cracked and broken seaboots that exposed the hint of dirty toenails.

"Ah Ha! The casket is amongst us me hearties! let's look a little further to see what's within!" said Peg his left hand, fumbling into his waistcoat pocket, his right hand still holding the telescope, still watching his crew.

From between thumb and first index forefinger emerged a grand key made of black iron and strangely shiny in places that gave an appearance that it had been constantly polished by his very hands.

He leaned forward bracing his wooden pin of a false let against the ship so as not to slip and positioned the key skilfully into its nesting place. On the turning of the key came back many memories to Peg of gold, of silver, of trinkets belonging to many kings but above all these memories came the distant calling in his crazy head - for TREASURE!

The heavy oak lid creaked and groaned open to expose many documents some of which were made from the dried skins of extinct animals! Some had been stitched and bound together to resemble what we can now only describe as books.

"Ah ha!!! I've found it!!" Said Peg arising up to spin on his leg in pure excitement. "This is the parchment I had forgot about having won it on a card game in the Bay of Shambles, where the loser went home to his family in a wooden coffin!!!"

The crew laughed and the seagulls shielded their eyes with their wings from a Captain who could be very cruel.

To be a Captain of a Pirate Ship you have to be a master to avoid a Mutiny and to have traversed the seas for three hundred years Captain Peg had become somewhat of an expert!!

Chapter 3

The Parchment unrolled looked bare, draped over the casket liken to an open table before that tablecloth had been laid with cutlery, long before even dinner and been served but to Peg well, he had developed a different appetite. He had a remarkable appetite to feed from Treasure Maps - and not fear hunger.

"Look here Norman, and tell me what you read" said an enquiring Peg.

Norman looked up. Norman looked through the hour glass with its grains of sand sprinkling to the bottom of another glass dome then said:

"It's true Master Peg of what you want, but I have cast these runes and the message is truly clear."

"And....., what's that all about Sawdoctor?"

"These runes are mischief, they say we will margin great profits but also they say that there will be a terrible storm. Look now! Even the sea birds have disappeared and flown to safer shores!"

"You have Norwegian Ways" said Peg, "You even told us all and one of a great flood but that never happened!!"

"Look now and look once more for I tell you that tonight it will happen!!!" said Norman clutching onto a small piece of timber with fear in his small but gentle eyes, maybe for real fear of needing a lifeboat.

"You talk in riddles Norman" said Peg.

"Maybe you have drunk too much Grog and if that's the case, then you will be bound against the ships wheel and flogged until you give up the true answers!!"

"But I give you my heart that this will happen" said Norman.

His feet curling and curling against each other, his body bent and open to submission. His hands glued to that very piece of timber that might keep him afloat, his runes like small plastic counters scattered around Peg's feet.

"I've heard enough of your nonsense" quirked Peg becoming angry form Norman's advice but in a strange way, still having deep respect for his only reader, even if it is runes.

"Go below now and write me a POEM" said Peg his left hand twitching against the unsure handle of his cutlass, and Norman was gone.

Chapter 4

"There's a swell on the Ocean
The waves are getting high
There's a portion of Norman's Notion
There is darkness in the sky"

The waves are getting so good that they want to beat you to death in this very beginning where all and one could lose the very thoughts of life. Rain lashes like a strop my father gave me when I had wronged and it was then that I, Chippy the Ship's Carpenter knew full well - that Norman had got it right.

Chapter 5

We never try to believe in Sawdoctors especially the ones that read the Runes. The ones that always come up clever at festivals, with their party tunes. Norman looked hard, then Norman looked at me.

"What's up Norm? Is there trouble afoot?" said Chippy with one hand on a sharp bladed instrument and the other on the stone that was honing its edge.

"Captain Peg has got it all wrong. He seems to me to be of much ambition" said Norman clutching a soft Muslin bag of Nordic stones.

"I often get that your feelings are true, now please give me a little time to help me in this repair of the life craft" said Chippy his tiring eyes looking up at a sky that was about to murder mankind.

Chapter 6

"The sea tumbled the 'Carnival'.
The sea rumbled the 'Carnival'.
The waters turned from black into white,
And all the crew hung on to anything
For dear life,

There is rain on the deck,
There are waves awash this deck
The ship is heavy in such violent weather
But the ship turns about in such a festive tempest
When even Sully the Ship's Cat
Turned around and scarpered
Underground to listen to heavens
Peeling with an unknown sound
Never given out ever until the Carnival
Turned its back again and ran aground."

Chapter 7

There was a terrifying crashing and grating of timber against sharp rock. There was a rocking and rolling as the 'Carnival' ground harder pushing forward until she came to a fateful stop leaving only an old oil lantern suspended on a lonely hook, spinning frantically as if itself was trying to grasp on to something solid.

All became quiet, save, for the wind still howling like a madman up and around the bent and twisted rigging.

"That was not just the Carnival being hurt me hearties" said Peg "It was more than that!!!, felt like the skin was being torn from my very back!!

No need to drop anchor. It looks like it's not needed tonight!" He turned around then tapped the end of a burnt out pipe that he was smoking against his wooden leg, the sparks sprinkling down onto the deck like the faint remains of a burnt out firework falling and fading away into the darkness.

The clouds flashed past the moon, but the moon seemed to be the only thing that was hanging on when everything on the earth had been tumbling.

Chapter 8

"Daylight comes to show to see
Daylight comes in that moment of glee
When sparkles in eyes
The pigs in their sties
Go sniffing and snorting
Under fair skies"......
"How are the pigs?" said Peg
"They're falling around a bit, I think they are still giddy Captain"
said Saviour his hands carefully clinging on to an old sow that
apparently looked bewildered from such a drastic evening.
"Go overboard to see what's happening first mate", and for once Peg
eased himself onto a small wooden stool and rested.
Saviour jumped ashore, turned around and shouted up to his Captain:
"Solid ground! Solid ground sir. We've laid up against a great earthly
mound of soil and up the very top stands a small tower, looks like
some sort of crazy Church. Further up this barren ground are young
maidens dancing in circles and chanting songs to the Earth Goddess.
What strange and canny place is this that you've led us to??"
"Tis land its true young Saviour. Let's get the men overboard to
check up and restock our small provisions" said Peg still somewhat
unsure of how to handle his eager crew amid young maidens. Having
been at sea for so long made the Captain feel even unsure about his
own actions.
"There is a small wooden sign here sir, it seems to point in two
different directions though, which one shall we choose?" said
Norman resting his arm on the stiled gateway.
"Tell me the meaning of this sign" said Peg.
"Well, to the right where maidens are singing with the flowers in
their hair it says "TO THE TOR" and to the left is marked in a deep
chiselled carving. "TO THE TOWN" at this sign's edge is a green
symbol unseen in any of the runic alphabets. it says NATIONAL
TRUST. We have landed amongst NATIONALS who are still loyal

to their King and Country!"

"I'll toss a coin and then it's up to fate of which way we go" said Peg spinning a gold coin high into the morning sunlight. Well, it's the town boys! Come on and follow me!"

Chapter 9

The men plodded off down a leafy lane roughcast with stones of many shapes and colours underfoot until they came to an obstacle that seemed to block their way.

A large crevice had been cut deep into the ground, its top covered with metal poles of a fine quality. Poles that some magical blacksmith had fashioned perfectly smooth and round.

"Be wary boys! For although this sign states 'CATTLE GRID' it could very well be a trap for fools! There is a small path on either side, take care, or else you may slip into oblivion!" said Norman carefully checking with his feet that the path was firm enough to withstand the weight of a man.

Further down into the town they passed an old building displaying a swinging sign above its dark and dismal entrance.

"Tis a recruitment house boys. Look at that picture of one of the kings soldiers armed with a very impressive musket. We won't be going there or else the press gang may bag us for the taking of a king's shilling!!" Peg had struggled for years to keep a good wholesome crew and no way was he prepared to lose any man now.

So they passed on by the 'Riflemans' and progressed further on until they found the town centre, a hive of activity, people going about their business.

"Captain look, a map!" said Saviour pointing to a large wooden board fixed to a post.

"It's a map and sure enough," said Norman "and what's more scary is, somebody is following us and has marked our position upon it. Look Captain it says 'YOU ARE HERE'."

"Quick Boys! Mingle in the crowd, I fear an ambush!"

Aware that there was no apparent danger of capture the crew spend part of the morning wandering the street sometimes picking up coins from hats that had been left abandoned on the pathways to the undertones of disgruntled musicians.....

Chapter 10

"I feel that these citizens have a fondness for the likes of us. Look a shop displays a sign for us and that I am sure of!" said Norman pointing his arm above the doorway.

"What's the meaning Norman!" Enquired Peg.

"Well, we came down from the Tor and this shop states clearly that it's a TOURIST INFORMATION CENTRE so I suppose that these natives consider us all - TOURISTS! Let's go in and make our visit!!

They opened the door and they all clattered in.

"Are you the tar men?" enquired a lady behind the counter, her perfume sweet and uplifting in its fragrance above the smell of a band of sweaty men.

"We madam are the Jolly Jack Tars! Thank you kindly for this warm welcome that your town has granted us and may the winds blow well on your next sea journey!" said Peg reaching out a hand to give a grateful handshake.

"We've all been expecting you now for some time and the Council have even provided us with your instructions. Here you are gentlemen and here is the map that you will obviously be needing" said the lady handing Peg a bundle of documents.

Peg looked surprised. His eyes lit up and sparkled even bluer by such an unexpected gift. He thanked her a thousand thousand times then shuffled his men out of the building to make a quick exit for fear that she might change her mind.

"Horse-less carriages everywhere, horse-less carriages all over the place! Big silver birds roaring across the sky but it doesn't bother these locals! They all seem to be unaware of these mysteries!" said a confused Saviour.

"They all seem happy enough not to bother at such things" answered Peg "Come over here boys to John's churchyard and let's have a good look at these new maps!" (His mind more focused on the papers held tightly in his hands, than Saviours obvious fear of horse-less vehicles!)

Ancient tombstones amid the grass makes a good meeting place. Ancient tombstones also make good seats!

Peg unrolled the parchment given to him by the kind old lady upon one of those stones and held the paper's corners fast with four broken stones to keep it flat.

"It's sure to me that this is a Council Map, and it's covered with lots of crosses! And lots of crosses means - LOTS OF TREASURE!!!" Squeaked Peg rubbing his hands over and over again, his heart feeling much lighter through excitement.

The men all gathered at the top of the town armed no longer with clubs, pistols and cutlasses but other more useful tools and equipment. Spades, picks and shovels now replaced their armoury and Captain Peg held tight to the most important thing - the map!

They walked the chosen route guided by a compass and the help of road signs until they came to a yellow marking on the roads surface that made the sign of a cross.

"Here's the first one!" said peg noticing that the ground showed some indication of disturbance for the surface was broken and pot-holed. "Start digging boys and above all, be quick and efficient in your work."

After a short while the ground was excavated to make a neat round hold but all was fruitless for there was nothing to be discovered.

"Make this hole good. Fill it in so well so that nobody knows that we have been here," said Pet disappointedly rubbing the dirt from his boots against the cutting edge of a spade.

They journeyed on they journeyed far down the roads and lanes digging and repairing each place that was marked with yellow paint, and each hole they dug was done so beautifully that their quest remained a guarded secret.

All the hot day they laboured hard sometimes taking rest along the kerbside to sup grog from an old oak barrel for refreshment.

The evening drew to a close. Up in the heavens the moon and starts were tucking the sun and light to sleep. The bats, the owls and all the night creatures came out of their hiding to feed and play and Peg's band of very tired men sat down exhausted to rest their weary bodies, their sweaty faces shining like little glow worms in the fading light.

They returned to the Carnival to collapse in hammocks and lay down to dreams that could change all their lives.

Morning came and once again they prepared themselves for another busy day digging and delving along the many highways and always repairing and making good any damage that they had caused.

It took three long hard weeks for the men to finally explore the last cross clearly marked on the road, as all the others once again they found nothing.

"It's a false map boys, I knew that it was too good to be true" said a disappointed Peg throwing his spade skywards until it landed in a ditch and disappeared under the weedy waters.

"Let's go back into the town and find a good alehouse and as you've all worked well I'll pay for all the drinks."

Chapter 12

The landlord looked up at them from across the polished counter. The landlord looked at a band of men in tricorn hats and swashbuckling clothing.

"Are you doing the Carnival? I hope it all goes well for you. How's the building work going?" Enquired the landlord rubbing the beer engine pumps with a old cloth.

"Yes good sir, we are from the Carnival but require some planks of timber in order to make urgent repairs ready for the forthcoming winter tides. My men need ale of the best - will this pay?" said Peg handing a solid gold coin to the puzzled landlord.

The landlord's eyes grew as large as saucers! A solid gold antique coin!!

"Have all you want boys and furthermore I'll get you all bread and cheese."

"Drink your fill boys" said Peg. Thinking to himself "How did the landlord know that they were from the Carnival?"

The return at closing time rewarded the crew even further.

By the side of the road was a large metal container full of materials.

"Look Captain! Planks of wood and stones!" Said Saviour.

"It must belong to a merchant seaman for the stones would make excellent ballast for his seafaring journey to the Spice Islands!" said Peg.

"A strange name though for a captain sir," said Norman, "it belongs to Southward Skip."

"Well at midnight send some men back here and take Southward Skip's timber," laughed Peg relieved to have found materials for the repair of his loving ship.

Chippy was busy, very busy sorting timber of varying sizes into piles and measuring each one before selecting the most suitable for repairs. There was ample not only to fix the damaged hull but also enough for coffins.

He had to keep busy because he had a deadline to work to. The winter tides were coming when the sea would rise high enough to launch the Carnival in Bridgwater Bay, November with strange bright lights in the sky guided him on his mission.

Four large wagon wheels had been fitted to the ship's hull so that eventually the Carnival could be pushed back to the coastline. Bright lights and thundering music filled the nights and it seemed to him that these were coming closer!

"Tomorrow night is the time when the sea is in and at a premium for us. Tomorrow night me hearties - we raise the sails and return to the oceans!" said Peg gaily dancing a hornpipe on the deck.

"How do you know that tomorrow is the best time?" enquired Saviour.

"There's talk in the town boys, they're saying tomorrow is Carnival night!"

Chapter 13

The ship creaked and groaned. The men pushed. The ship eased forward. The men pushed harder.

"All aboard and raise the sails" shouted Peg down to his crew.

The wind grew stronger and filled the sails and the Carnival slowly moved forwards to the sounds of creaking wheels.

Down to the town they progressed past the Rifleman's recruitment house to the top of the high street amid the cheers of thousands of people that apparently had tuned up to wish the men well on their journey.

"Wow," said a spectator, "Look at that! It's so good that it looks like a real pirate ship!"

Everybody cheered and the crew waved. Some in fun waved cutlasses and shouted back pirate type gestures.

The Carnival was almost sailing! It rolled along the road and out of the town. Along the Polden Hills it progressed until it came to the edge of Bridgwater where in the distance could be seen shimmering waters of the sea.

The moon was up. The tide was up and the Carnival gently settled her body safely on the water. The wind billowed the sails, the ship lurched forward gathering speed and then in the dark night - she was gone!

Apparently the ship won first prize but nobody knew of any Carnival Club that had built such an exhibit.

"It was almost like a ghost ship" the people would often say as the years past and the distant reminder of the Jolly Jack Tars moved on into Folklore and history.

But who knows? Maybe one dark night there might be a knock on the door..............

Blind Self

I could not see myself today, The Great book of Order - had followed me in my discontent. The book I believed in, was hollow. I read a passage and saw a sermon. A time to think, and think of you.

The Brook, the Babbling feeling of not knowing the distance between life and death.

The distant between longing; And on Age, knowing slow death.

Give me one drink, make me think; of world disasters then turn around, to give me a chance to believe. In an old world you only saw, In a moment, my troubled thoughts.

The bark still grows on trees. The light is blind at this hour, when, we see visions of newness and Crazy things in our drunkenness....

The bank still grows on embankments of disorder. Where snowdrops cover themselves in shadow. Who are we now in our slippers, looking up to the cocoa-mug to, even think, we are human.

I put my hand on my heart to say -, "I did not know!"

The train to nowhere was cancelled.

Snow on the lines

My eyes also failed the lines

That's when I found the answer -,

I needed new glasses.

Pleasure

Wow! -, I am ordered!
No longer now the journey
It's still forgotten somehow
But in that dream - when he took over the bed,
I got a stange feeling that he was wise.
Think, teach in me and I shall allow you everything
Detentions at Midnight were my cause,
I paused,
Then looked around at your naked beauty.
And she laughed - no tease or pease
I play the laughter it makes me think,
Of the key -, that you gave me,
And how I laughed at that.
When my troubles were elsewhere and you, my Swedish friend
Were darning the carpets.
Why recall that moment when we are here and now -
But, why again - do you repeat yourself?
My life was full to the utmost of pain.
The warmer winds never changed me -
Maybe the winds were too dry?
But I always remember soft summers
When the cows were sucking grass.
Lowlands -, do keep moisture to add to any drought, so why the pain,
I asked?
Pain is something else - another journey.
You are younger to even explain its mystery.
Which mystery lasted?
The one when the coin was spread,
Upon your very table.
With the ungiving hand - the one

Who spared your thoughts to forgive me
As I returned
          From journeys far.
Everything explained, although far fetched
Maybe I need more time to understand or
You do not bother at all.
Why bother! When this changing wind
Becomes my new maker.

Keeping Score

Teacher handed back our work
Sat down shuffled feet and mark book
Selected her weapon
This time it was a pen
Called out our names in Alphabet order
Which puzzled me to think -
How are we all born in sequence?
Why am I always at the bottom
Feeling lower than my score?
       Cricket came with the weather
The usual forecast with rain
The spin-bowler's arm finished me quick
A jerk good enough to break a rabbit's neck
My father would have been proud of him
The beauty of being last man in
Is being last man out
The beauty of playing football
Is studying the goal posts
You have to as all goalies do
I spent my life looking
At other people's scores
I knew I had been chosen
To do something useful

Letting Go

When there is no more to give
No one now to love
Let these coffin bearers carry me also
Down this very aisle
Where we both walked hand in hand
When we were younger
Didn't know too many quarrels
Or worry about the next settee
Semi detached or tailor made
Like this box you reside in
I knew this person well
The times good, bad or indifferent.
When the smiles made me laugh
Like also the hangovers
When he would curse the day
           Then get on with it
Red letter days and birthdays
Times when sometimes I would see him slip
And almost expose
The true identity of his troubled soul
Yes he was my lover
Like no other he knew how to handle me
And in so many ways lead-reined my spirit
To compete in this world filled with tenderness
He wasn't the best mediator - far from it!
Only one king can rule the kingdom
And by golly I come to believe
That in those lonely thoughts self-consuming.
He owned the world to complain so often
That the tenants never paid the rent.

The Meeting

On a Saturday after cleaning out the cowshed, and bedding down the animals I was paid. This gave me the chance to visit the cinema in Street.

When she came I thought it was all sorted. That idea that your very parents made as they looked down on you with their knowing gaze, - I thought i was happy.

My own father not being disturbed by the tobacco-tin, a present from his own father as he fumbled a short piece and hand rolled it into the well of an empty pipe.

I thought my heart was full as my body had been in the 'Flea-Picture'. When Mrs Evans always flashed her torch into the back bays of seating - when she herself was doubting us, as we fumbled looking for the popcorn and lost ice-cream sticks.

Lights on at the beginning and I was still blind. Struck blind from the Big-screen and its purpose. I immediately thought I was that very hero until I walked out into the light and the very fight that was not prepared.

A Bish! And a 'Bash' until I found the answer to the combination-lock that held me fast from escape.

I cycled home to the tunes of the music as the credits rolled in my head and I myself felt whole again.

Further I went as any man lost in gain. Further out the space, when so many before me learnt to be young again.

Walton is an easy village. It has no meaning. Past the church with its interesting history on the left but I myself was pushing pedals. The hardest part of the journey home to Shapwick village was in two clearly defined stages. Two steep gradients of road, one at the Piper's Inn Freehouse and the other coming out of Ashcott past the Millfield house sporting beautiful young girls in bikinis. Girls so wealthy that they rarely showed any interest in a boy that had no more value than second-hand goods in a charity shop.

At the top of Shapwick Hill where the view showed an almost lost valley that stretched far away to the soft grey colours of the Mendips I had a strange meeting.

She was sitting in the back of a car looking at me. Her parents were looking forward and they were eating sandwiches. I wasn't sure what was in the sandwiches. I was still spellbound by her presence. She looks just like a girl I'd been watching that day at the cinema.

Fay Dunnaway in "Bonnie and Clyde". A younger version though but just as beautiful.

I paused to take up a foot upon my pedal, still looking at the most beautiful thing I could ever gaze upon. She stayed in the same space, mouth apart, half-opened with a sandwich likened to my own mother's biscuit tin. When, if you're only good then maybe _____ "Here's one for you".

Romance comes unrepentantly, like bad news or rain. Romance is a strange feeling when you were carefully nurtured and educated to a point when you thought you knew all the answers.

The girl was still looking out from the door window, bemused at my struggle to continue my journey home. I was still enthralled at the fact that maybe I'd just met a filmstar! The bike eased forward and I free-wheeled down Shapwick Hill to my home village. I never saw her again.

A Child's Memory

"The Fast and the Harvest": The Irish Venture
The time of a great famine - and the English didn't care

The fields were cleared quicker this year. A year of drought when we as youngsters failed even to notice the sharp blade of a scythe that never really had anything to cut against. Wild grasses against the wild roaming weeds.

We were dancing, dancing in our dreams about a better world that in our sweet innocence we never knew anything else than to just dance among the flurry of dandelions so soft in their touch as the Candlewick bedsheets that kept us so much warmer in wintertime when the frost was speaking.

Little bread on the table next to the mantle that held a glowing ember of warmth. Little bread for hungry bellies and I was sure -, to be correct - there would be at least 'afters'. Perhaps an apple pie from our forest of fruit trees but no, that never happened.

Afterall what would we expect? We had to sell our produce that was our livelihood. The harvest had failed. We could all learn to understand hunger tonight and bless the day that God sent us. We all prayed and prayed hard.

The rusty implements said their own kind of story. No more bread and we all learnt to be hungry again. No more to turn to our own master and ask him - if the world is right to say: "Just give us a pasture, a little more work to harness you in your majesty to your horse and plough - Regardless of our plight".

We resulted to collect acorns to make a coarse flour in a bid to stave off hunger.

We all rummaged amid those trees, oak trees so ancient in their glory to allow us a simple task - to collect the very fruit of those boughs. So simple are we. Simple no different than our own mother who was cooking up our tea and with the other hand making a small hand-stitched tapestry of how we made the journey home. A small decoration of her thoughts and inspiration written with a needle and thread of a time when we were still out chasing the last Pheasant into another kind of wilderness.

To challenge him when he became cornered. Kill him with a big stick knowing he could not escape amongst this forage that to us - is the moor, amid the overpowering bracken.

I like pheasant meat far better than Acorn Bread. I know no distance but to say today that in my heart we all ate, and tomorrow well who knows what is lying dead in the wire-snares that we set well yesterday? The wire snare illegal - but never mind. Those braided wires that we stole from the local electricians store shed. The very traps that would always work.

We'd make them like a hangman's noose - the slip-knot guaranteed to restrict the air flowing through the neck. The oxygen to the brain would be denied and whatever was trapped - would be dead. Die in agony - never mind.

Sited too near to the village we snared a few domestic cats so we prepared them in the fields. Casting off their skins and guts into the ditches where the rats and foxes would devour all evidence. Cats that have been skinned taste just like rabbits (cats stripped look like rabbits). Their stripped bodies look the same so we ate them. The neighbours ate them also, and wondered what happened to 'Arthur' or 'Jenny'?

We decided to live. That was not hard. My younger sister had caught the great fever and she died. She was laid outside the Churchyard having never been christened. We all looked up to God in those grey days when the moon wasn't looking too good either. When the eventful rain came it flooded the graveyard again but this time it washed away any evidence of her resting place.

The flowers that we as infants had placed upon her became no more than a slimy wilt of yesterday. The flowers are no more, no more than the difference between land and space - the very difference between Ireland and a possible home-land in an afterlife.

On a still day or maybe a troubled one when the mist finally cleared away, when we all were doing our best, the soldiers came. Dressed in a uniform that we were not accustomed. Some were armed with rifles. We were armed with rakes and spades but they didn't appear to notice the difference and caned us hard with their butt-ends. Invaders to our country. Invaders true until we told our fathers over supper and then there was a war. A war that still hasn't been settled. A war where we blame anybody but ourselves. Some sort of crazy argument that could never be settled over a cup of Mother's tea and a short-crust biscuit.

A Statement

"Here I stand the Smith.
Who searched hard to find the philosopher's stone.
But instead, found a treasure so great, that
All I could do to show my lowly worth
Was to model her into a wife."

Into The Night

A conversation with a troubled friend

'Twas a still night, short of restlessness. She steeped her cloak down to settle upon our land. A land that was ours, always retained for the next flurry of mankind to come and maybe feed these Marshland birds that will always sing their own stories. This sky brings upon us many pleasures. It also brings the tales of suffering that we, as youngsters would one day come to learn and talk about again when we got a little colder to the weather.

My friend became my common enemy because I loved him too much to question his thoughts and feelings.

My friend looked at me and maybe I turned to glance a parting blow of his thoughts without speaking aloud. I knew he was hurt or seeking some incredible, solution and so, I kept quiet. (Keeping silent sometimes works).

He talked of rainbows, home-cooked food and a flood of butterflies that might come if the season got warmer.

I mentioned colours through prisms, a recipe book that always did the business for me and that the weather showed some promise to settle down, just like the dog dreaming at the hearth.

"You can't be serious?" said my friend looking harder into my face that I almost thought that I was made of glass.

"Hang on" I said "I am feeling a bit brittle". I could see some angel or another breed that does the clearing up tenderly brushing up my soul that had betrayed my body underneath and had scattered on the tired ground.

"Look outside" I said. At that moment a great God in heaven made one of those very interesting lightning bolts. "Just look at that!" I exclaimed feeling inside as if I'd just fallen from off a swing.

"Life is so golden!! Why sturn your head into some sullen pocket.

When all about you is this terrible night that causes many firework parties. Don't journey with me in fright - STEP OUT INTO THE NIGHT"

After The Pub   2006

She came
Breathed a soft sigh against a neck
Smelt smoke in my hair
Cuddled closer like a hungry anonaconda
Just wanted to be there
Wanted in a loving way
To share.

Caught a dream of mine
In the folding of her hair
Asked me straight – what was I thinking?
Something told me deep inside
Do I dare?

Do I tell her my thinking
The raptures of my bottles in endless drinking
The lies that line the wrinkles on my face
The unsteady walk at Hometime
With an equally unsteady pace?

The Foundling

I can full remember my application form. It puzzled me so much that I showed it to my teacher. A man who had no surprises so much so - that I respected him. He wasn't the sort of guy who would openly put me down in front of the company of anyone. He looked over the form and with some help assisted me with the big words that he knew full well I'd have trouble with.

The dust in the playground tumbled up into a small cloud as he started the engine of the ancient car that he was proud of. A car that was his usual vehicle and we often wondered if teaching was a well-paid job.

I was eager, as any young boy and sent the letter away carefully dressed with a first-class stamp. (The teacher had given me a direction 'No first class stamp - no action!')

The weeks rolled by so slowly that for a moment I thought that he had let me down, until one morning there was post for me!

I ran to greet my parents into the warmth of the kitchen that always serves a hot meal and told them that I was going to join the Army.

Silence is sometimes golden but that was shouldered to a pause until my own father took it upon himself to cause civil action.

"Well done Son," he said. "It was better than messing about with a skateboard and annoying the neighbours".

Mother took it badly for what, I failed to discover. She just kept very quiet as she lay the dishes upon the table for another perfect family meal.

We ate together as a family and by the time we had finished my loving parents had eventually come to some agreement, I needed a career.

I remember clearly the fumbles of Mother as she insisted on packing my baggage. I remember the look on my fathers face as he checked the life-blood of the dip-stick in the family car to prepare for the long journey. Then I was gone. Today I was treated differently.

So many roads to the place of my dispatch. I saw so many beautiful flowers and also of my own love for those I'd leave behind.

The great engines turned and fired up into common practice. The wheels of a great aeroplane moved down the blackened runway and slowly left the ground to feel fresh air against those hot tyres.

A soldier is born. Complete in the correct dress. Complete with a firearm of which he received little training.

The landing was just as bad. We all know the differences between good suppers and nightmares.

Still thinking of our Mothers and that long journey home to our own fireplaces with maybe a candle that always lit our thoughts.

Life has adventure.

The sizzle of tyres upon a new found place. The sky looking similar to my love for everybody.

The platoon sergeant barked a command and we all responded.

Discipline is very much different in the regiment. Always obey orders and no excuses for those who feel forgetful. All punishments are severe but also life-saving.

I remembered the guidance that my teacher had given to me as he shook my hand with a firm grip. A grip that was a mark of faith in all people.

"Promise me one thing" he said as he stubbed his cigarette into one of our potted plant pots.

"What is that sir?" I said.

"Learn to duck and try not to be a hero" and then he went back to fixing our broken toilet pan.

The back-pack is heavy and the boots rub away the human in me. Never complain because you don't want to be a "wimp" and even better – let your team down. Far out into a crazy desert I was taken hanging on tight to my seat with knuckles shining as white as that very candle my mother had lit for me.

Our camp was a bit basic. It was a million times worse than any school camp where all the teachers had made perfectly sure that we were not really suffering. Suffering now was the meal of the day and it looked like the menu would never improve.

The night is clear. It reminds me of so many other calm nights until the flares were sent up into the heavens and we all thought it was Bonfire Night again.

An attack! And the bullets were very real smashing the brickwork so much we all thought the demolition gang had returned for some mad rebuild. I wondered how my friends were doing and in the same sentence they were probably thinking the same about me.

"Man down, man down!" somebody shouted and in that decay I went to offer assistance and then for some reason that I could not explain – I was hit.

Not feeling too good today. Feeling a little strange until the boys fought hard to pick me up and drag me back to the enclosure.

It all happens here. The Medic tried to stem the flow and all I could see as I looked out from tiring eyes, were my family and my hometown.

"He's gone" the Medic said and I guessed very badly that the chips were down and I had to forfeit my life.

The plane arrived down on a similar tarmac and I was overboard. Given a hero's service with music but I knew I was dead. The good man being carried now by his friends that were always taught to show no emotion, no feelings about a brother lost.

And they laid me to rest.

A hero born,

A son that you looked up to,

A foundling.

The Woodlouse Farm

- Based apparently on a true story

Chapter 1: "A Simple Life"

Harry Little shovelled the waste from the chicken sheds, resettled his pipe in his toothless mouth. Fumbling for the matchbox he settled a hand on the shovel and the other stubbed fresh tobacco into the almost rimless bowl. An old pipe puffed by and even older man.

The smell of the chickens and the rising stench of creosote from the rotting timber-framed buildings, reminded him of his life. A simple farmer whose wife collected the eggs each day in a pinny and oversized Wellingtons. It wasn't so much as growing into the boots, age was taking its toll and now she was shrinking out of them.

The hens knew her daily visits. At first sight of her headscarf and the rattle of the metal bucket brimmed with corn they'd scurry in hoards across the barren field to greet her and eagerly feed as she, the provider would scatter the grain amongst them. Breakfast was served.

"It's best to feed them early. They lay tastier eggs" she'd say to herself. Who knows the answers to farmyard traditions?

Harry loaded the wheelbarrow and proceeded to hobble across the bumpy field covered in tractor ruts to the far corner bounded by several mature plum trees. He spread the manure around the trunks.

"Best food for plums. There's no better fertiliser for them" he's say to himself, his pipe jumping up and down in his mouth as he said each word.

A farmhouse in a mundane village where nothing really happens. A place rarely frequented by tourists unless they're lost on their journey's to better places. They may stop at the crossroads to set directions totally unaware that all road-signs in the village had been altered by mischievous village children. Maybe pause to look at the ruined, neglected church with its grey slate roof peeling with age and its tower clock pealing a call to Father Time. A place where even the lichen covered gravestones leaned against one another for support amid beds of stinging nettles covered in crawling masses of butterfly larvae.

A farmhouse with a clutch of acres of ancient pastureland completely untouched by modern husbandry. Organic as every egg, every chicken dinner and every man who grew up in the community.

Harry and his wife were contented. Their bellies were full and a small amount of savings had been hidden away for the "rainy day". Maybe no need to store money when so many previous rainy days hadn't bothered them much.

The vicar was a madman. The Reverend Price was a dangerous man, he owned a large motorbike. A big green noisy thing with a loud engine. Up and down the country lanes he'd ride as if the very devil was chasing him.

"I don't understand him wife, I don't know what's come over him. The last vicar had a bicycle and he managed to get everywhere on time. He wasn't even late for Bill Dyer's funeral and he wasn't too sure when he was going to die" said a very puzzled Harry scratching his head while holding his pipe.

"He'll come a cropper one day and then he'll know it!" said the wife. "He won't be going fast then... you mark my words". The two of them both nodded in mutual approval and carried on working.

Farm work is hard and there are no breaks. No holidays. Barely time to wash and shave. The seasons bring their own kind of variety but at the day's end work still has to be done. Being born into farming the Little's never knew any difference except when there was a glut of fruit at harvest-time and then everybody worked even harder.

They had no off-spring. Harry knew of childbirth. Over the years he had witnessed his animals screaming in labour at the joys of motherhood and assisted as a well-trained midwife would. He had even reached far inside a pregnant cow with a full arm and tied a rope around an unborn calf's hooves so that he could pull it out into the world. Difficult births apply to all creatures. After such a turmoil with the aid of his wife they would swing the still body of the newborn calf around and around as if it were part of a skipping rope. Doused with hot water, doused with cold water then Harry would kneel down and push his fingers up into its nostrils to remove mucus and clear the airways. Most people would have easily given in and accepted that the animal was stillborn - and at least he hadn't lost the cow. Real farmers are special. They never give up and as usual the baby would give out a cough and feel born and wanting its mother.

Drenched in mucus and water Harry could then watch his newborn suckle up to its parent.

Yes Harry knew of childbirth. That was his reason for not wanting a son or daughter. He loved his wife too much and the last thing he'd want is to watch her suffer at his expense.

Chapter 2: "Morning Has Broken"

Blue skies above. Sunshine brightly reflecting from a loose galvanised roofing sheet hanging from the barn waving gently in the faint breeze like a fan panning the warming air.

A ball of small kittens rolling about in play. Chasing each others' tails amongst the hay.

A banging sound from the bottom shed - Harry was fixing the tractor.

A small twang came from in under the engine cover and Harry looked up to the god in heaven as if to give out his blame.

"What's up? Harry? Are you okay?" said the bewildered wife.

"It's okay wife" - he paused for thought - "It's only an airlock again".

The corroded fuel gauge had long time lost its glass cover and subsequently lost its indicator needle which resulted in the tractor running out of diesel. Harry had topped up the tank but now had to manually pump the fuel through the pipes to the injectors. A ten minute job but only with the correct spanner!

The ignition key was turned. The engine spluttered gasping out thick fumy smoke from its upright exhaust. A second attempt and the tractor fired back into action.

Hitching up a small trailer that was laden with empty cages he plodded from out of the yard to the chicken field.

There had been a few poultry problems recently in the form of 'hen-pecking'. Hens can be very nasty sometimes and pick on certain victims. It's a bit like playground bullying in the schools and can lead to mortal consequences. Hens that are constantly picked on can often die from their injuries. Farmer Little used an old farming tradition which although drastic and barbarically cruel - always worked.

Amid the clouds of dust and feathers fanned up in the scurry to escape he caught the main ringleaders and caged them up. Boxing them up onto his trailer he then proceeded to journey back to his timber-framed workshop where his equipment was set up waiting his return.

A workshop full of bygone tools, parts of horse-drawn equipment, rusty dusty tins of veterinary potions set solid amongst the growing layers of thick dust on the undisturbed shelves. Somewhere further inside on a workbench by a dull window webbed with spider curtains an area had been carefully prepared. On the surface lay a rusty metal box and in the box was a heavy copper-tipped electric soldering iron shimmering with heat.

Harry grabbed a chicken then with his other hand grabbed the wooden handle of the hot iron.

The smell of burning bone filled the room like the smell from any dentists chair when they're drilling out cavities. Harry was performing the lost art of 'beak-burning'. This involved removing the sharp stabbing point of each offending chicken to prevent them from causing injury to the weaker ones that lived in the pen. Yes, it sounds awful to think that the birds suffered a torture but it was a remedy that always worked so was still practised.

At certain times in the year when the grass had grown taller and was rich with seed caused another problem for Harry's flock of egg-layers. Chickens can be useful lawnmowers and are prone to feast on these dry seeds which can sometimes result in them becoming 'crop-bound' which can also result in deaths. The seeds build up in their necks and get stuck there. A hen affected by this condition becomes ill and has a tendency to fall about as if drunk.

The solution to crop-bound hens involved a delicate but effective operation. A sick chicken would be held down which was relatively easy as it was dying anyway. With a single-edged safety razorblade a small cut was made to the swollen neck area and using a finger the seeds could be scraped from out of the hole. With needle and cotton a stitch was made to seal the wound. Once the chicken was released it would stand up and run off to the field with no apparent side-effects. The perfect cure and no need to knock it on the head to put it out of its misery.

Chapter 3: "News from Nowhere"

The Reverend Price sat in his lonely office in the vicarage looking out of the window at the red-bricked boundary of his enclosed Victorian garden. Looked at the ripening plums and yellowing pears and wondered which village boy would dare this year to scale his wall and take his crop. It happened every year and even when those bad boys grew up to manhood the vicar knew that their off-spring would probably carry on this illicit business. Looking up at his three-dimensional portrayal of Christ crucified at Calvary Hill he said a little silent prayer to himself hoping god was listening. "Please God, let them leave enough for the Harvest Home celebrations at the autumn service. Just enough to dress the church altar. Just enough to make my church smell of produce rather than the wax polish Mrs Fisher leaves behind after cleaning.

He leaned forward over his desk and reached for the 'Parish

News' leaflets that he had been preparing. A mention for the Women's Institute coffee morning, the monthly church service diary and this month a special urgent request - fund raising for essential church repairs. He knew Mrs Little would willingly assist him in his work. She was a regular church-goer and without her presence in church on Sundays the congregation would have been halved.

To raise money for these church repairs the Reverend Price had decided to work closely with the local primary school by holding a fete on his vicarage grounds. Any profits made would be shared equally between both church and school. After all the children did need a new football. The last one still remained lodged in the corner of his guttering and had gone green with algae resembling now a grotesque gargoyle spilling rainwater everywhere except down the waste pipes.

The Reverend Price sipped lukewarm tea from a vacuum flask as was his daily habit. He was busy and didn't need even the whistling kettle to disturb his thoughts. He mused at the plastic and chrome container, a gift from his beloved father when he started his studies in Oxford all those years ago. A flask as sacred as his holy orders and sometimes more meaningful than religion itself. The teachings of Christ the redeemer seemed less important to the newcomers to the village who preferred to be served in the pubs and polish their posh cars instead of attending his sermons. He thought "who wants to go to church on Sunday especially after such a heavy Saturday night drinking the latest cocktails?"

The postman arrived and pushed the bulging mail through the letterbox. Mail that fell onto the porch tiling amid the leaves that the wind delivered also. Reverend Price eased up from the leather-buttoned armchair adjusted his spectacles and collected his letters.

Pamphlets for hearing-aids, double-glazing, and a large brown envelope with a government stamp on.

"What's this?" said Price, "an important correspondence from the big city. It appears to be very, very important - this paperwork looks expensive!"

The paperknife slit the throat of the envelope open and out poured some ugly news. The government had compulsory purchased an area of ancient land next to his village graveyard for new housing developments. This cannot be - this cannot be. That very piece of land contains the mortal remains of many ancestors. Why, even the Strangeways are interred under that very earth and the Littles are distant relations to them. It was the Strangeways who built this very village many centuries ago from their success as sheep farmers and even to this day Mr Little is allowed to graze his own sheep there. "I fear this will cause much upset to this peaceful place."

That morning the Reverend Price made a great number of frantic phone calls. He rang around his diocese! He rang the Bishop and even an old scholar in Oxford but all hope was gone. The planning had been approved from some grand city dwelling that knew no better than to sign documents. White-collared workers who had never even seen the serene beauty of a village lost in time.

Reverend Price sat back heavily into his chair and wondered how on earth he could break the news to his people. How could he dare himself to tell Mr and Mrs Little?

Chapter 4: "Bad Moon Rising"

Mrs Little went as pale as the handful of eggs that she was holding. Harry Little looked unusually angry and bit down hard on the stem of his pipe that the only sound audible was when it gave in under his grip and made a large 'CRACK'!

The Reverend Price sat silently sipping the hot tea that Mrs Little had freshly made and all he could offer was a comforting hand.

"It's not your fault vicar, I knew something like this would happen one day. I could almost feel it coming but what's more important now is the meantime. We've a village fete to sort out and the youngsters would be all disappointed if we didn't just carry on. We keep this news to ourselves and see what happens later" said Harry and for one of those rare moments he put a warm arm around his wife's shoulders.

"Yes," said Price, " we will endeavour to carry on and do our best."

For one of those even rarer moments his silver crucifix was seen to slip on his neck almost transforming into a distorted shape.

Chapter 5: "The Preparation"

The months passed quickly. Mrs Little had busied herself hatching out eggs in the paraffin fuelled incubators. Constantly checking each egg marked clearly with an X and Y. Each egg turned daily to ensure effective hatching.

Harry helped the Reverend Price by moving the heavy wooden trestle tables from the cellars of the village hall to the vicarage lawns.

The school children were buzzing with excitement. They had been working hard making fancy dress outfits for the future competitions. Mums had boiled jam pans almost dry in the rush to display their expertise and helpful fathers had erected cloth marquees around the grounds.

"So much to do, so little time" said the pretty school teacher who lacked so much experience but had a head of golden hair. "The preparations are going very well Reverend Price" interrupted the head teacher. She had so much knowledge that she could have published books just for extra-curricular activities like village fetes or even growing herbs.

They worked hard as a united group for everyone desired a success. They worked hard half-believing, it was worthwhile.

Completion almost to the very mark that 'Price the Elderly' had made on the village before his last return to missionary work in Darkest Africa and no news of his return, or where he was?

No calling from his wilderness unless the swallows had told this crazy world anything differently when they themselves prepared each other for the endless flight to far off lands.

Chapter 6: "The Long Wait - and Then the Fete"

"Look at me mummy - I am running!" Said an excited boy who had dropped his computer game to run wildly across the lawn. His egg in hand, held by a mysterious invisible spoon had stayed in its correct position by a somewhat strange event of nature called cheating.

Nobody noticed - nobody really cared - This was real entertainment!

The swing boats swung, the children ran, and all that could be seen was a perfect day. The tiny children spent many fruitless hours searching for 'The White Elephant Stall' but only found tables covered in sell-by-date tins with raffle tickets stuck on them.

The tea flowed to its last trickle. The jam and scones were sold out and the prizes were share equally to all competitors so that nobody left disappointed.

The posh cars revved up into action and everyone returned to their homes and their white-collared jobs. Mrs Little and the vicar counted out the money, to share with the school. The pretty school teacher offered to assist but admitted that maths wasn't her strongest subject blaming it on the colour of her hair.

The beautiful bunting adorning the trees appeared to wave goodbye as the last people left the site. The Reverend Price sat back in a low stripy deckchair, reached down for his flask and poured out a cup of lukewarm tea. Mr Little lit his pipe and wondered how on earth it had been damaged?

Chapter 7: "The Builders"

A large yellow digger with a sharp front loader scraped the green face off the field. The builders had arrived excavating the land by digging out the foundations for the first thirty new houses. The quietness of the village now became disturbed by a huge company of workmen making an incredible mess. The country lands became scattered in yellow clay from the constant removal of unwanted material. The builders in their high-visibility jackets didn't seem too bothered to keep the village tidy. They had work to do and deadlines to keep.

A large green motorbike spluttered to an abrupt halt at the entrance to the Little's farmstead. The Reverend Price dismounted, wiped the mud from his protective goggles and walked across the yard where he found Harry sat amongst the hay in the well-stocked barn feeding the owls with the remains of Mrs Little's unhatched eggs.

"Good morning Harry. My you certainly take great care with those owls. How many have you got now?" enquired the Reverend Price trying in a way to distract Harry from the lorries that rumbled by his property.

"Sixteen this year vicar. That's eight broods from these owl-boxes I made last summer" said Harry pointing up to the top of the barn where his nesting boxes had been carefully installed.

"And, how is Mrs Little?" said the vicar.

"So, so... She's keeping herself busy" said Harry in a low voice.

"I've got to go somewhere this afternoon. You couldn't keep an eye on her whilst I am away. I'll be back for teatime." said Harry

"No problem" said the vicar "Why I'll even help with the chickens. It's been a long time since I've handled these creatures".

"We are all God's creatures aren't we?" said Harry releasing the last fed owl to flutter high up onto its roost.

Chapter 8: "Harry's Plan"

The clock in the village church whirled inside its stone tower and struck six times against its metal gong announcing to the public that it was teatime.

Mrs Little looked up at the kitchen clock and wondered where her husband was? The potatoes were peeled and were simmering on a low heat on the stove. The meat was sizzling in the oven and all she had to do was open a tin of peas and wait for his return.

A sound coming closer, a familiar sound of the upright exhaust pipe and Harry drove into the yard tolling a trailer that contained a large wooden crate marked clearly with a sign that said 'THIS WAY UP, CAUTION LIVE ANIMALS'.

"What's in the crate, Harry?" enquired the vicar.

"Come and have a look" said Harry.

The Reverend Price peered through the air holes of the wooden crate and exclaimed "It's, - it's an anteater!!!!"

"Yes vicar - and I am calling him Alfie" said a proud Harry.

"But, but what do you want an anteater for?" said the bewildered Price.

"I have a plan" said Harry.

"I am sure you have a plan husband. Now come on in and have your tea. Are you staying also vicar? There's plenty for all of us," said Mrs Little reaching for the can-opener.

"I'll be delighted to stay. I am getting a bit nosey - now tell me Harry - what's the plan?"

Harry left the peas on the edge of his plate. He never did appraise tinned food except for corned-beef at Christmastime with the crazy wire key to unwind the top and then call aloud for the plasters in the First Aid tin.

The vicar ate all his meal, even the peas. He didn't mind tinned food especially being hungry and knowing Mrs Little was a very good cook.

"Now Harry, what's this plan you have?" said the vicar staring hungrily at the green peas on the edge of Harry's plate.

"I am taking up a new farming venture, you could say that I am diversifying. I have decided to start farming woodlice."

"And, what is Alfie going to be doing?" asked the vicar.

"Controlling them of course! With the correct training I am sure the anteater will make a good farmhand".

He laughed, the vicar laughed, Mrs Little laughed and for the moment they all shared happiness.

The following morning Harry got up early and eagerly walked down the yard to the large crate. He unfastened the wire hinges and opened the door and there looking up at him was the long snout of a very large beast. A very large anteater!!

"Come on Alfie - work to do but breakfast first" said Harry and Alfie plodded out of his cage and followed him to the kitchen. With specially prepared 'meals-for-one' anteater and other snacks sent from Bristol Zoo, Harry made sure that his new pet was okay. Alfie's long snout hoovered up his meal and when he had finished he plodded into the sitting room and lay down on the carpet in front of the glowing embers in the fireplace. Farmer Little suddenly got the strangest feeling - maybe Alfie might need some serious training..........

The months went by. The intensive training continued. Alfie proved an expert at rounding up the farmer's livestock and boy could he run! The lively anteater had boundless energy and Harry looked proudly at the pet that had become a close companion.

Things played heavily on the Little's hearts. The building work by the church was completed and new people were settling into the village. People who were strangers to this once unspoilt place and showed little respect to anyone else who lived there.

"They don't even come to my services" said a sad Reverend Price, and even more disturbing is that some of these new boys are stealing my crops!! I have nothing to show for my efforts except for a few withered fruits that are still clinging to the broken branches. They've even damaged my walling".

"Don't let that worry you vicar. I have a plan," said Harry in a reassuring way. "Come over here to my sheds and have a look at what I've been busy doing".

At the bottom of the farmyard stood four very old and unstable wooden sheds that had once been used for rearing young chickens. Harry pulled the unsteady doors open and the vicar looked inside. The sheds were full of wet rotting logs and timber, the faint aroma of dampness filled the air.

"I fail to understand you Harry" said a bewildered Price holding a white cotton handkerchief to his nose to filter the overpowering stench.

"Look closer vicar, look closer!" smiled Harry and paused to light his pipe.

"Woodlice! Woodlice!" exclaimed the vicar.

"Yes vicar - woodlice and furthermore - millions of them! Now listen to me for this is my idea".

The plan was simple. The Reverend Price was to deliver leaflets to the residents of the new built houses. Nobody would suspect him so he would prove a good messenger. Not only was he to post his godly words but also something else. Harry had prepared dozens of white envelopes and inside each one contained a few hundred of his tiny creatures.

"Sprinkle each packet through their letterboxes and we'll sit back and watch the reaction" said Harry with a cheeky look in his aging face.

"Why?" said the vicar as he viewed each small package to check that none of the contents was escaping.

"Just do it" said Harry rubbing the long snout of Alfie who was also peering into the rotting log piles.

Chapter 9: "The Curse"

The local newspaper headline said it all.

"A PLAGUE OF WOODLICE - ARE THESE HOUSES HAUNTED"

The Reverend Price was interviewed by a young spotty reporter who offended him somewhat for as he asked his questions he continued to chew a mouthful of gum.

"Yes," mused the vicar "It is a pestilence as written in the Holy Bible in Revelations!"

"Then, the houses are really cursed vicar?" said the boy almost choking from the obstacle within his spotty mouth.

"I fear it is the wrath of the Almighty. These houses were built on sacred land and the ancestors buried within are obviously fighting back" said a concerned Price as he fumbled empty white envelopes upon his study desk.

"What can they do to lift this curse?" said the reporter.

"Attend church on Sundays and ask the Lord for forgiveness" said Price

That following Sunday the church was packed with a large body of very worried people.

Chapter 10: "Price's Sermon"

An old green motorbike pulled up outside the church entrance. The Reverend Price noticed many cars blocking the way and as he approached the church door, no longer did he smell Mrs Fisher's wax polish but the mingling perfumes of many well-dressed females.

He stood straight and walked into the building. The church fell silent and all that could be heard was the sound of leather vicar's shoes on harden flag stone flooring.

The vicar's sermon was full of fire and brimstone and lasted a long time. Within his lecture he mentioned that a great beast with a long snout could save the occupants from the terrible evil that had fallen on the village.

"I know the answer to this problem" said Mrs Little as she shuffled pass so many people. "There is such a beast that lives not far from here, do you think it could help?"

"We shall see this beast and its owner and pray to God for our salvation" said Price shutting his bible with a loud snap.

Chapter 11: "Alfie's Mission"

Harry had decorated a small trailer with coloured bunting and old Christmas tinsel. On the trailer he had positioned a grand chair and on that very chair sat a very large anteater!

"This is going to be a costly business" said Harry.

"Whatever the cost we will pay. We can all claim the money back from our household insurance and the builders have offered to pay half of the bill" said the worried residents.

The tractor fired into action and Harry journeyed down the lane to the development adjoining the churchyard. "Come on Alfie - do your work" said Harry.

Alfie jumped out of the trailer then posed for photographs. He then proceeded to visit each afflicted building and with the aid of his remarkable snout hoovered up all the woodlice. Licking his lips with an incredibly long tongue he jumped back on the trailer and posed for even more photographs.

"Don't pay me" said Harry "give it to the vicar as this money will be spent on urgent church repairs".

The church was repaired. The congregation continued to attend the Reverend Price's sermons in fear of possible future infestation. Mrs Little opened another tin of peas and Mr Little and Alfie? - Well they had work to do, there were other housing developments in the area and an anteater would always be in demand!!

The Moth Inspector

This funeral has reached as far as this hanging rail - where I keep the suits. Carefully filed as papers and important documents in my metal cabinets.

The mice only ate my Manuals! - they knew I had better answers. Why they didn't eat or make nests with my own handwriting God only knows? But the Moths had harvested my Suits. Clever Moths that were fully aware that I didn't go to meetings anymore so all suits were dispensable.

These moths are big. They threaten me. I've watched them walking about in the bathroom using the shower and even more annoyingly - my shampoo. I have little or no control over them especially the Boss Moth (He doesn't take life easily). That huge insect is in charge of all natural woollen materials, even my favourite Mole-hair jumpers that I adored; They happened to be presents from my dear Mother who usually had such bad taste with fashion.

Last Sunday evening I arrived home too early and interrupted one of those 'Moth Meetings' that they usually had every other Wednesday. How was I to know that they had skilfully changed the normal appointed date? There had been no message left on worktop or fridge door. Nevertheless it made them cross so they retired to the back room then turned their furry faces to sneer at me. Somebody is taking over this house.

I sat downstairs in the kitchen. Up above me I could hear the eager munching as they polished off my dinner-suit. What was I to do? It wouldn't be long before I'd have to walk the streets of Glastonbury naked (as if it would really bother this community).

The light of this day was drawing in and everyone in this street were drawing their curtains. I couldn't - I didn't have any. They had simply disappeared! I blamed the lost on my lodgers at first, until i realised I had other company in my home.

There was a fluttering noise coming from the front door knocker. I wondered who on earth can this be at such a late hour? It surely could not be my neighbours. I didn't have my music on. I eagerly paced to that dusty wooden door. Maybe it was that pretty girl I'd met in the cafe and she'd suddenly changed her mind! I opened the door feeling a different kind of flutter deep within my heart. Standing unsteadily on two of its chosen feet stood an enormous Moth dressed in the finest draperies. It was the Moth Inspector. A very difficult breed even at the best of times. I let him in and he just turned his head - and looked at me. Going upstairs he examined the threadbare carpets, the holy clothing and drooled at the ceiling light burning bright.

Within the distant room I could hear him shouting at the Boss-Moth and the stamping of at least a half a dozen feet. There was a great commotion. The bedroom door opened and they all marched out of my home. They had been evicted! No more food!

The last I heard of them was that they were all hovering around a streetlight at the bottom of the street, just waiting for someone's window - to open.

There's a Christmas Luxury

There's a luxury in town tonight,
A super smooth penthouse party at Christmas;
Where everyone sips French white wine.

In pseudo cut-glass
To peer in ecstasy at 'petite fours'
Through thick, sickly smoked glass.

Where each decoration lies in place,
"LOOKS GREAT"-
      Over the plastic fir tree by a bricked-in grate.
In that room with a constant heat,
They talk of central heating,
      which you just can't beat.

There's a real luxury in town tonight.
In a red bricked house,
In a red bricked row.
Where people just come and go,
Their hands and fingers all aglow - icy bitten by the snow.

The trimmings in a puzzled heap,
The dog that just lays fast asleep to gently growl with firelight's heat.
And as each log crackles bright,
The candled tree stands proud alight
The smell of smoke that fills the room,
      Far better than Chanel perfume.

The Christmas spirit only lasts so long
In a pseudo world I don't belong

For all it holds is a plastic smell,
That came right from the mouth of Hell.....

Moon

How graceful could you be,
You waning woman,
That scars the clouds of heaven?
Looking down on misery,
That thrives another day,
You shelter in the sky,
To see me through the nights.
And though this storm may rock you around,
I'll see you tomorrow.

July '78

Father

Dad said things just like they are,
A passing light of a distant star
And,
Then he was gone again
A passing noise of Shovel
In the distant Rain.

He had a fatherly look,
Wiser than any book,
But,
Deep in his heart my Mother took
Something that left an Empty Space
Those days when his eyes looked so Blank
Like when he'd insufficient Funds,
Beside the Taxi Rank
He'd look at us and say "Never Mind"
We saw a man locked in Time
He'd turn and think awhile
Then tell us that in everyone
There is always a smile.
Even from his enemy's grin,
Nothing seemed to bother him.
He was my father he was 'dad'
Even on days when his eyes looked Sad.

The Craftsman

I am the maker ------,
That is to say that in me all things are possible.
Let me take you to a woodpile
And say "this is not firewood
But a store of hidden furniture ----,
---- It only lies as waste to an unseen eye."

Lazy Fish

The fish were droozing
In the sea,
A fisherman came by.
The fish looked up
And saw him there,
His face against the sky.

They swam, they swam
They swam away.
They swam from his great net.
The fisherman leaned overboard
And found the water wet.
"My Gosh!" he said in great dismay
The fish then stopped to look
The net came round them underground
       And all the fishes took.

Today with Memory

Today with deep regret,
I heard on the news,
That Popeye had died.
      Olive cried.

He was a bit old,
The cancer they say
Had entered his liver,
And ate it away......

Today with deep regret
Bruto ruptured himself,
      It hurt.
It hurt so much,
That he bit out his tongue,
Whilst holding his crutch.

Today with relief.
Little weed was raped.
      It shocked them.
It really shocked them!
And they still don't know if it was Bill or Ben?

Today on the Riverbank,
A tale was told,
Roddy Rat drowned,
      So sad.
It was a hot day
So he jumped right in,
And soon he found he couldn't swim.

Today in Poggle Wood,
The poggles were shot dead,
    A tragedy.
Rumours in town,
Say the A.R.P.A. (Always Ruthless to Poggles Army)
Had entered by force
And killed them of course.
And Candlewick Green,
Will never be seen,
Cos they're all blanked out,
In a radiation screen.
Trumpton 'le Somme'
Dropped an Atom.

Today Mr. C_____
Was drained of all Blood.
Sooty thought him a queer
For fondling his rear,
And ripped out his throat.

So tonight when you're sleeping,
    In your beds, snug and tight,
Sweep will stab you "goodnight".

A Day's Fishing

A morning sky was stippled by low cloud and I had no doubt that it would be yet another hot, scorching day. Earlier that morning I had cut cheese sandwiches and prepared a flask of tea for refreshment during my days fishing. Humping the heavy fishing basket packed with a jumbled mess of tackle boxes, ground bait and sweaty worms, I walked the road to the river - my secret escape from a working life and nagging people.

The tall, octagonal stalks of white headed cow parsley leaned over the road almost shaking hands with that, and the sour smell of hot melting tarmac mingled with its scent which pinched the back of my nose with remorse that such a sweet smelling day could be ruined by mans achievements in road building, for to me this was a flag day for Nature and there was an affinity so great between Nature and I that we were inseparable.

Buttercups shimmered softly in the meadows and daisies were in such abundance that they resembled layers of snow or maybe some deserted beach on some foreign shore.

My tackle box chattered away in time to my footsteps which distracted grazing cows. They stood chewing the cud watching my progress and occasionally leant down and licked at salt blocks, their tails whipping pestering flies from their backs. They constantly licked dribbling, runny noses longing for a shade to shelter from the blistering heat. The elm trees that once stood proud like ranks of uniformed soldiers had suffered greatly against the battles for freedom against the Dutch-elm disease which had severely damaged the face of Somerset. Their tall, skeletoned, leafless bodies barely hid sufficient shade for the shadows and poppies blushed in the breeze at their nudity.

As Us

How can there be any sorrow,
In two as us.
We strive to win, In all we do;
No - matter what,
We still pull through.
Where pain out wins the honours,
We still fly our scarlet Banners.

Out in the field,
Knights fight in the wind.
And with our love which is our shield,
We all go out,
       and win.

Bright Sunlight burns my aging face,
Yet to this tabard gives it grace,
"You must be bold" she said.
"The flame of Hope that you cling to
Is a fire that I hold"......

Like lead, I felt Blood drain.
Glanced up to you I felt no pain.
As just before this dawning hour
You gave to me your scarlet colour.

Far on the fields they saw,
What they would die for
For we are two when they are one,
And as this Battle surges on ---->
    I know I'll see a new day's sun.

Moving on against all odds,
My Horse forgets those weary plods,
Rears up his golden mane,
His heart a-turned to flame.
Straight although its startled face,
Kicks up with hooves far into space.
And though they fell far short from sun.
He knew that war had just Began.
A truly trusty Steed,
As love outgrows the Wisdom,
We rode to find new seed.

yes, where each man stands
the test,
I know I was the Best;
And when the Devil called his Host,
I know I killed,
          the Most.

Waiting   1982

I'll wait for you,
At a place where hedgehogs sleep
Curled in leafy blankets
I'll wait for you.

I'll wait for you.
In shade from summer evenings
Where honey-bees no longer look for flowers
But drink a dewy nectar
Where your footsteps marked the ground.

I'll wait for you.
Through branches skeletoned behind this glassy moon
That never waxes
Yet wanes its sullen light for want of your affection.

The Artist   '84

I've sketched,
but could not capture your beauty
My colours are here
Drying and fading on this pallet.
But yours
Are bright and ever-changing
They defy our mortal spectrum.
I am staring and thinking to Copy you
But the image is moving
These clouds keep changing
As the mood that stirs me into
painting the impossible picture.
Yellows now turn - into Orange
As the Sun begins to set
And the blueness is gone
And greens turn into grey
The shadows of early evening now taunt me
As your colours fade away

The Rod Master   '84

Here I sit
A master of my Art
Watching the sun chasing o'er
Ripples of untroubled waters
This shade feels cools and soothes me
Yet the river,
She crawls in this heat
And there about me
In frenzied surprise
Minnows and fry at play
Are dancing beneath my feet.
This river she plays a sweet tune
Of unwritten music
Yet never to forget the scores.
As reeds and trees join in the chorus
And sunlight gleams
My thoughts pour forth,
In flowing realms.
I'll chance to cast again
With a fear of weeds
One whip of the rod and the bait flies true
amidst a burst of dandelion seeds
That drift away and drift along
To find a place where they belong.
I've waited and as always I wait for you girl
With the shiny tail and loving swirl
A smooth firm back and dark brown eyes
That lives deep within this paradise.

First Thoughts of a Day   Feb '79

I awoke this morning and although my eyes were closed I knew it was a beautiful day.

The sun shone pink pastel shades against my eyelids, warming my whole body, brimming my soul with pleasure.

Nothing seemed important and in those few brief moments I gain a satisfaction that no other pleasure could relate.

I lie perfectly still. As a boat upon a lake I let my mind and thoughts drift away into hidden fantasies and endless streams of vapour form shapes of all I desire.

The beauty of all understanding lies hidden in these moments...

The light swims more brightly,

And I awake.....

I am not an Angel

When I was little,
I had feathers,
Thought myself a small bird.
But I grew old amongst Angels
I know this sounds absurd.
I lost my buds in schooling
Denied the gift of flight
Learnt the rules of Mankind
Forgot the Animal fight.

Mr Jones   Nov 1977

I am a modern classed tramp,
Eating cheap newspaper cuttings for breakfast,
Then spewing them up over
My 10 o'clock break.
I am friendly for liaison work - but don't ring me after six.
My IQ rates high I wear a bowler but not only that
My armpits smell
My sub ordinates all three
Call me a man
They respect and bow low - I don't think they talk,
Behind my back
I am very intelligent
Languages actually 'I speak three',
All of them English of course.
Some Sundays
To dear mama I take the wife
She loves the kids all
Planned of course,
We got married first
Rich
Rich am I
My rates are high with the food bill added
Yet sometimes
I wish the rent was monthly
For convenience
Of course
I haven't many secret admirers
I don't need one,
I have myself....

The Sunset of Undying Love

Here is the sunset of my undying love,
The colours of my life will only fade without you
And leave a world stripped bare of emotion.
I gazed upon a skyline, once green with a treeline,
That stretched into a haze
And I thought of love,
        and its endless limitations,
I stared up unto a sky and felt a pity,
For those birds lost in their timeless flight
and I pondered further on this timelessness in my own flight,
But it is here, where I find just one more glowing facade.
My love for you abounds
And it is filled with a richness
likened only to the ripening of a good fruit,
Or the sweet smell of the springtime
That has the power to cause all things to change.
There are many things that although withered, cry out,
from a frozen ground to force and burst new growth.
My love for you is never forceful
        Its in a natural state,
But like the trees upon this skyline,
There are times when its colours are strong,
        Yet today we are looking too far,
        and can only see the haze......

The Consequence of Thought

What have I done?
Sounds like I've set off a gun,
Made you afraid in your bed.
I should have stayed silent instead.

What did I say?
That made this summer grey.
Made you walk at a distance from me.

How can I tell you?
How sorry I am, you the one,
That found a kind man in a fool.

The kind of light
That settles down on roaming hearts
And History
Reflects a passion of lost suppers
That you my sweetheart could only ever,
Bring home to me.

Loss and Gain   2007

To suffer loss when loved—,
And miss it.
To clutch a faded photograph—,
And Kiss it, —,
            as a hole bore through the Soul.
Nothing more is lost
for feelings never leave
Nothing now remains
Save time to grieve.

To suffer departure
and Know
Something that was once yours
Has moved to another rapture.

To run a finger through her hair
The comfort from loves departing—,
Is holding the memory there.

Holding back feelings
By biting on a lip
But pain tries to extinguish love
In its strangling grip.

The lightness of feet
Chance meetings in the street
Quiet corners within rooms
Fragranced airs from soft perfumes.
Pub singers that got far enough in life
To be served at a bar,

A few free glasses then a
Passing wish to a distant star.

To feel a need and openly say,
Your life is filled with disarray.

To hold a dream and clutch it —,
Then lose Friday in a crazy head-fit,
To find enough strength as you stand —,
And reach out fingers, — to a hand;
Catch a laugh together
No matter what the weather....,

Give up on the memory
Of having sex upon the sand—
                    or the moments when you doubted me
Forgetting shelter from this aging tree
Cut me down - then left an Open space
For this cruel wind
To once again Rape me.

The doves that sing only bring
Dust upon a folded wing
And though joy was greeted with a smile
You turned your back and thought awhile.
You turned from me and left me cold.
My hair grows grey - as I grow old.
As old as the tubers found
Hidden in this loveliness ground.

The Piper played as you danced
You conjured up a New Romance —,
Lifted feet above the rising tunes

Spread your seasoning on Desire
Cast me in Brimstone and Fire
Giggled as a young girl with a new Toy
Left me alone again to remember
The Boy.

When men laugh at my expense,
The anger raises to intense
Purposes of Words and Feelings —
Beer flung high all over ceilings
      — a drunken man with senseless reelings.

And when the heart is breached
When all good leaks out,
That's when you stand outside
You hear my shout,
As I lick open wounds
Under shade of changing moons.

The meanderings of the rivers and the mind
Wrapped up in the glossy web of Time
The look that you gave as you parted
Not knowing of the war you'd started.

The lightness of feet as
a first performance on a stage floor
Re-evaluating our loss
With nothing more
Than the emptiness of hearts
In the closing of a door.

Nights filled with lost Passion
To the edge of Reason.

Comfort comes with the warm hand.
and,
Sexual gratification turns into a Sore.

She came — (they always do),
A silent flicker on Clitoris with tongue
That uncoils as a spring when Sprung,
Circumvented breathing
As decay is heaving, —
                    up against belief.
The Great Organism, — and then relief
A deep sense of calm
As if my soul was rubbed in Balm.

This Night is calm so calm indeed
It draws me down in its shadows with depression.
I could have been good.
Thought better before the uttered word.
But I was bad-blood—,
A useless folly
Liken to the ones that stand in the Woods.

No, I wasn't born to grow old.
Lost fortune has little place in this town today —,
But —,
        to lose love means to me
No more sunlight dancing on the Sea

Ummm..... 2007

A phrase is a group of words
Although this sounds absurd.
Like 'under the tree',
Or 'under the sea'
I feel these words mean little to me.

A clause is a group we project
And consists of a subject
Joined up with other groups intense
To make a single sentence.

Age 2016

The sight of an older woman's legs,
No longer excite me
Please wear leggings
Open-crotched
And
Keep them on so that I can pretend.
Of days when
Everybody was made of Silk.

The Child 2014

Safeguard was always one of those words my parents never taught me. They were safe, and as far as that goes they were always on hand in my hour of need. Nobody really troubled me apart from my own thoughts which to so many others could turn up and become a real problem. Life has so many highs and lows that I almost felt deep down inside that there was no single soul who could ever offer any help.

I read the books from jumble-sales and even when they were half-read somehow my Mother removed them to the dustbin. Too much clutter in a hamlet of farm cottages that knew no more than the four seasons that make up a year.

"You'll get yourself in trouble by reading those things" said my Mother. How would she know? I had been reading. I was almost finding my way down the River Nile or some other delta. I was at home. At home sitting in an old chair by the Rayburn heater wanting to talk to the exposed springs of a seat that kept me awake.

Winter comes and winter goes. The only difference I could honestly see was a change in what we were wearing. Winter, lots of clothing. Summer, a time to show more modesty. A time when the sun burnt our skins more than the low burnt fires of December.

My father came home tired. He'd been working on the peat moor. He was his usual self by that I am stating that during the working week - he was tired. Covered in a black skin of dirt so deep that he had to scrub himself at the sink into the white-man I so much respected.

Life goes on. It continues like the noise of the water pumps down on the distant moor.

Draining away so much fluid that without its help I may well have been born an amphibian. Some wretched newt with no more worth than to be speared by village children as a crazy form of entertainment during the summer months when they are all trapped in the enclosure of the village pond. I should have been speared then but instead because of my infirmity, I was spared. Spared to be bullied later in life but I knew of answers that they didn't. I had been reading.

Not the leather-bound books that one finds in an old museum. Merely the worn-out covers of others misgivings. I did not choose the titles. I was grateful of being allowed one small chance to make futile progress amid a community who failed to even notice.

Weather Forecast

Here I am an old man
In a white month
Where the very seeds turn to despair
Of what is now holier,
      Than taken in the air.
June came with a promise -
June failed to keep it -
I asked the Weatherman for an answer —
And he said straight to me that is was Isobars?
Funny lines that obscured the map of
The face of what we stand on.
North winds from the South,
Wildebeest winds to the North.
I wondered a long time —
"What was wrong with Seaweed?"

The Illness   2014

Yesterday was much the same as other days. Even when the worm turned within the giant machine in the factory or the other packed his/her suitcase and left me to eat from my garden in the morning, with the restless songs of blackbirds competing against one another to eat my thoughts.

I couldn't sleep. The blackbirds had finally called for me to get up, arise and make vain attempts to find two matching socks. A cold shower and the North wind came and reminded me that it was still winter. Where is that remarkable thing? I don't really know. Where is that plastic thing to scrape across my innocent face to remind me that I am only human?

The doctor arrived early and told me it wasn't looking too good. I looked around for good, but suddenly realised that he was talking to me. I never did like the way he dressed - too formal, so much so that I was equally surprised to notice that he had rested his tiring bones on one of my dirty chairs. He must have been tired or maybe he himself was thinking of joining me and giving up.

The slight moment when he dropped some crazy medical documentation on the floor, to retrieve it and rub my house on his right leg made me think a little bit more of how filthy my home was. Nectar over-brimming as pollen on so many forgotten flowers.

I often wondered about this medical profession with the weird white-coat workers whose only interest is to pack you off to somebody who he thinks he himself also is a specialist. Don't believe in white-coats or even white-collared workers who never seemed to lay their hands on Mother Earth to dirty them to belong to me and my fraternity.

Mother rang and enquired about my health. Like a liar speaks, I told her that I was okay and had been given a clean bill of health. Minor problems so small that a bit of medication couldn't sort out. She sounded happy. So did I biting my tongue to suppress my true feelings.

The cat came through the small trap and looked up to my amazing face. He also seemed to ask the same questions so I lied to him also. A good cat, almost the person that i should have married all those lost years ago when the world believed in me. Some cats have thoughts. Mine just have inhibitions that makes them so much more worthy.

The clock is ticking and the music is just the same. Noting changes. I don't need a weather-forecast to tell me it's raining outside. At least it cleans away the dog-shit that often litters my doorstep.

A sudden twang and a sharp pain reminded me that maybe I was a little bit unwell. It made me see stars and for a brief moment I felt giddy. Just like when as a small boy I experienced the same feeling on the first roundabout in a park in a town also littered with paper scraps and somebody else's dog shit. Where is this pain coming from? I never harmed anybody like this so why does God think that it's funny to play such tricks on me? Another pain so I made a small coffee to give some other extremity some kind of warmth. I re-marked on the label on the fading coffee jar as it didn't belong to me. Just like father's whisky bottle all those years ago when I thought it clever to be a grown up.

The doctor gave me a small white plastic bottle to pee in. I wondered? My willy isn't that small and how on earth could I piss in such a small hole without making a mess on my hands or even more - the floor?

For a brief moment my hands were warm and the carpet below oozed to a darker colour. Ever changing just like the smears on this bathroom window that always fascinated me. A work of art that really belonged in the Tate Modern or maybe,-, just my window.

I crippled up and bowed my legs to admit defeat and submission. Rocked a bit and nodded at the W.C. The small receptacle that flushes away all debris. Is it at all possible to remove this obstacle within me? Nobody was interested or even listening...

This staircase gets steeper each day whether up or down.

It turns into an achievement that I wondered how much it would cost to maybe employ a Serpa from the distant lands of Nepal. I don't thinks a Serpa could stick it for too long and he'd give up and go back climbing mountains for a break.

What's on the television today? Another antiques programme and I sit here so old and worn-out that maybe I'd need some careful restoration or better still - a true evaluation. Life though is priceless but we are all replaceable, regardless of how indispensible we feel. That's life. Just like a burning candle that gives off light everything eventually has an end. I just wish I'd been told when it all started at this moment of my departure into the great unknown. I would have taken better care of myself.

Something inside told me that it's kicking. If it hadn't been for the fact that I am a man I would swear that I was at least six-months pregnant. This though was a different kind of lump that would never require the help of any midwife.

I had a lump many years ago. I fell off a swing and banged my head on the unforgiving tarmac. It was the size of a small hard-boiled egg but it got better. It went away. I think it was only a borrowed lump and reserved respectively for the next child who dared to swing 'hands free'. This lump I have though is a part of me. It has decided to be cloned on my person without permission just like the unexpected guest who turns up at my dinner party knowing that I am fresh out of chairs to annoy me so much that I'd have to eat standing up and watch the vain audience devour my efforts without complaining. Life is kind. It's a strange discipline to announce to anyone your true feelings about anything these days.

Are we too vain to say that sometimes we are immoral? Too cocksure to admit we all have a common weakness or better still a common enemy?

Another burst of pain put me into a spasm. Stars in my eyes again that I thought of ringing Patrick Moore to tell me what constellation was in my head today.

Thirst comes and goes. Coleridge must have felt the same when he wrote 'The Ancient Mariner'. He was on some form of opiate as well.

I felt sorry for him.

Today I sit in the same space peering through jaded eyes at a fading photograph of my children when they were younger and believed in my stories. Today I sit in this same space and people tell me that I am a chronic alcoholic. I'll drink to that. Self denial is only a word written in a textbook.

Just Passing through

They lit a candle when I was born
A light into this world

I met you in the Sunshine bar
A strange light shone in you.
You asked what I was doing here
I said "just passing through".
This liquor it does things to me
It makes me think anew
Of past loves lost and holiness
And all my good times too.

The Sea 1979

The sea-surf laughed and gargled in
Upon the sifting sands,
The waters turned renounced a cry
for spirits in the sea.

Those rocks they jut like parapets.
Driftwood cased in foam and snails
Bash against its rocky flails
And rancid weeds of many kinds
Go sifting through the slipping shales

The waters turned renounced a cry
For spirits in the sea.
Immersed with spray a wave goes by —
A flap - and seagulls flee.
To weave and mourn for empty thoughts,
Their flecked plumage climbed.
A widow wading dress rolled up,
Watched them all go by.
A thousand prayers and whimpers there
Had gathered on the shore,
The tides had changed and once again
Returned a thousand more
Straggling strands of greeny slimes
Snake their ways through murk or clear
To seek for some stone to adhere
Until the torrent turns away
To leave them high and dry
Baked in the sun so dry as clay
Until the surfwaves roll them on

The surfwaves roll on, on
A hollow drum had washed ashore
With lowly muffled haunting call
As if a church behind the hill
Rang out its distant mourning bell.

Let Nature kiss that dying breath
So she may rise again
The surf-waves roll the flaking sea
The surfwaves roll on roll,
Where sultry salty fishermen
Their faces stained with sweats
And lifelong days down in a hull
They cast crack waxened nets.
And looking up from under caps
Squinting at the sunlight
Between one's teeth he held a grip —
A horny wooden, rumpled pipe.
All sailing out to sea
Or will it be deaths door?
Far in the morrow deep with sleep
Bring fishes to the shore.
And laughing at the catch may even
give a sigh
But now they wave a gesture
Or had they waved goodbye......

The Passing of the Life of Heart   29/3/06

On March — 29th
Your letter made a solar eclipse
For a little while
The world went darker
And the birds were quiet.
The black clothed bearers
Brought the hearse outside my door
Broke my kneecaps
So I could be fitted easier in the oak box
And in doing so
Denied my ability to walk in the afterlife.

Blue lias path slippery
They weaved footsteps into the fabric of a life
Often haphazard
Misguided, misinterpreted.
Tried their best to avoid cracks in the pavement
For fear of this earth swallowing them up
Clicked heels in time
To the distant din within the building huge
Of some old biddie badly fingering the board
and misreading the score through old spectacles
Of a sombre D minor fugue.

Aunty Molly came
Wearing her funeral hat like a scripture
Uncle Arthy walked more upright than usual
Carrying a Picture
Of my life in crazier times
When I crashed his treasured possessions

When he trashed my arm in cidered sessions
And told me straight!
       To get my life in order.

With one more River to cross
All I can now see
Is a wide foreboding sea.

Sprinkle Confetti on my Grave
For a Marriage born in Heaven
Sprinkle onions on my Liver
For those meals you'd dutifully deliver
Cast the sea salt to protect my soul
From your favourite Bronze-wear bowl.

But then let me tell you in tenderness
The nettles grow upon me as wilderness.

Your letter spoke of love
As a four-lettered word
Like pain, like hope, like gain
And words with more than three syllables
As denial is a river in Egypt.

But what of love?
When it's held by the pallbearers glove
A flash of white cotton under these morbid skies,
In this graveyard where love itself dies
Becoming more and more neglected
As a road-kill covered with flies.

In this very church where I was born
Baptised and given a candle to hold

Listened to the wedding bands
And the wailing of the bells in the tower
Held a wife then slipped a ring
On a loving finger in a terrible din
Gave a blessing to a Godson —,
Not that I remember him.
Gave her my blessing when she parted
Wrote a big cheque not knowing what I'd started
Not realising my fate
In spilling communion wine on her mother's dress.

The notice on the locked church door
Told me God wasn't home
Told me not to steal the Holy service
Said another scripture
A parable of wine and roses
I'd wish to meet those Bishops
Stuff faith right up their noses
As in the Whore houses and card games
They dealt
Whilst all my family came to pay respects
Of a man's decaying body
And how it smelt
Of Sandalwood and labour
Could offer them my simple sermon
Of an afterlife —,
          and how I must refrain —,
I would come back again.....

They turned heads upwards
And witnessed the moon scrape its face
          across the Sun.
I knew they would blame me.

On Sunny Afternoons we used to wander
Far away, up over the Quantock hills
Watched a deer or two
Bobbing asses through bracken
Like me and You
Romance is bliss
      and tenderness
Usually starts with a kiss.

That's right - carry on, step on me......

Smiling for Sorrow   1982

You come to see me,
And you make me happy,
My smiling mystery.

I'll chance to wait a future call as tonight
When we squashed our bodies close
In an empty pub
Thinking of lonesome fools
Buckled by the bar talking of boozy nights
And summer girls
Dressed in white cotton
Or was it cheesecloth?
I wasn't listening.

You watch awaiting
My first rusty move
Of rather slow disconnected movements
That rumple blankets,
Without harmony to my wishes.
You're thinking of lost values
Or was it homework?
I don't really know
I wasn't listening.

Could I just say... for the sake of old values
that we could smile for second thoughts
And draw upon this moment as yet another mystery
In the game of love.
Or are you just a questionnaire
That cannot be completed through lack of answers?

We don't really know
We're no longer listening....

Home Brew   2016

It's playing me up again —
The Homemade
So I drank it all to Change the World.
I sorted every problem
By writing them down
You came to ask me
"Are we going to Town?"
"To the Pub?" I said,
No, shopping instead
I held out my hand to feel hers near.
But she gave me a bag
"To hold more beer?"

The Changeling   2006

I got up and changed my spots
Wore a different animal skin
Crept upon the loose ridge tiles
and cowered in the Night.

British Summer Time changed an hour
In Greenwich where the bell
Wept in its lonely stone tower.

We drank coffee
By the church square
Sat amongst the office workers
Also sitting there
You readdressed my shirt
Then rearranged my head
Told me that I was someone —,
But, I was someone else instead.

This temperate weather
Overcast with rage
Washed the streets of litter
Brought us back again when you said
"You're no quitter"
For all this world's worth today
I failed to measure you
Calculated your eyes and legs in movement
Held your heart and soul in lost evening's spent.

Are we Sure   2005

Insecure tonight.
I've watched your fumbling,
From the nice bag with mirrors
That your mother bought you —
On a fancy
Knowing full well
She'd forgotten your birthday.

Unsure as you spilt a little
From a full glass
Unsure,
          As you made a tittle, to turn around me
As I passed.

These are the simple things
That cause enquiry.
These are the hopeless smiles
That can only be written
On the odd toilet wall, or two.
Man is nothing more than an adventure,
Some strange geographic map of excitement
Liken to a foreign journey.
A packaged holiday
Before the real stealth tax was paid.

To Follow in Her Likeness   1981

Nature is my mother
And like a sheep within a fold
I shall follow her forever.
She uplifts my spirit and draws my fading breath,
So as for one more brief moment
I can breathe the very air that sustains the soul
And is life-giving to all unborn things.
I say her changing moods are womanlike,
They cope with more than mortal man who
changes his values to suit himself — and
shows bitterness when he has wronged.
She cares for the frail and feeble fledglings
In copse and for those that live high on mountain-sides.
And of the trees deep within the forest
That never see the light of day
She draws them upwards
To feel the sun's caressing rays.
There must be a place for all to thrive,
And a home for each one.
The insects that live under stone,
The larks that like the meadows,
And the fish deep within the sea
Are all a balance without which if one were gone,
Then the rest would perish also.
I shall learn to know her ways
For I was born eternal young.
The scholars say that wisdom comes with age —
But even I have seen an old man die,
Knowing nothing more than to be a man....

An English Woman Abroad

There she goes
That girl with coral sand 'tween her toes
Wrapped in a Kaftan
With the sun and the smiles in her hair.
She bleaches the surf so soft as this sand
With the cares of the world
Wrapped up in her hand.

They say she had a private life
An ordinary way
Rusting with her rustic man
She walked a solitary figure,
Collecting bread and bacon
And lived in her icy silence.

I hear her skin is going brown
Coffee coloured as this mug in my hand
But I know her as my Englishwoman
Although I had forgotten to be
Her Englishman.

Departure 2003

On going,
As you leave the door
Silently closing the latch
So it doesn't wake me
Slipping back into your high-heeled wake
Letting the crimson dawn
Stand and stop
Surprised by your actions
Turn around and conjure up
The clouds into deeper blue.
You would not surprise my thoughts
If I, in sleep had awakened... —,
I would have stayed lying face up
To the ceilings
Of all the promises I made
In tightly folded fortune cookies
In my head and sighed...

No more does she come,
With warmth against my neck in slumber.
The stills slowly fermenting, breath
Barley grain on cold cellared floors
Ooze out their feeble offerings
From yet another unforgiving summer;
And the brewer lets it slip away
From the tired press in his tired hands
And who will know?
Who will talk about us at dinner tables
With the correctly folded napkins
Standing like solitary nuns?

Running fingers over and over the cutlery
And being excused of which
and what spoon
To use first.
The tapping tinkle of a spoon
On the rim of balloon glass and be speaks again.
Not again, I thought.
He likes his say
But only in front of dumb audiences.
Does he perform his chosen magic
Like a lion-tamer with chair in hand
Asking the dead lions for an opinion?
Or is he afraid?
Lions are like these wetland adders.
They only die at Midnight.
And me?
I too reincarnate also at Midnight
But with the same all too familiar face.
So as not to disturb my friends,
My family.
They would only wonder
What the fuss was all about...

The Wetland

An Angel Watches Over Me

The field it is bare
Naked and exposed to the wanting child.
Let the ball roll
Or throw it high!
Loosen your limbs and run through this barren wilderness.
Stubble like prickly heat or a nettle rash
Rubbed sandaled feet
No dock leaf was there though to rub
On skin and leave its browny walnut stain.
Far out, let me take you even further
And see this sky so dark on a distant horizon
Subdued by the clouds, the silhouetted clouds,
The stones and the sullen ground.
Can you hear that whimpering whisper
Of reeds fighting upon this wetland?
She sifted softly sliding down the silvery stairwell not knowing even
the heat,
Of a journey into Hell.

Her garments followed each tread in spiralling waves
I couldn't see her legs, lost in flowing movement
The clothes remain as her linen,
Fetid and soiled, and sifting rather than
That graceful smack that fresh cotton brings
upon the breath of one who is not liken to laundry.
When the light is fading gently with a certain
Eloquence only challenged by the day.
And that great ecliptic shape is lost in

darkness, pray let me go a wandering,
Near the mirror of brightness
That makes this old canal cling to me
In arms we may stagger with age
And unknowingly walk on coarse
gravelled stone, grey with its squalor
And foot loose uncertainties
Along this channelled neglected railway lane
My heart is caused wander from the footpath.

This stillness remains sacred, undisturbed in
her beauty she, this Heath land can only arouse in her sleep
As fishes rise and predators splash
Rippled rings lazily follow the shallow pools
And silhouetted shapes of waiting Rowans
Dance with gaiety upon the surface.

I was graced to see the swan
The shining bird in her purity was equally
graced to cast an eye
With no turning of head
She lifted a blackened leg webbed and thrust
away in disregard to my presence.
A wave, strong and rhythmic
followed another but she raised her neck aback
And showed her downy wing and glowing splendour before resting
Near the duckweed small and spinning
in her wake.

The song I heard bared little to
Its true meaning
I climbed down the staircase unseeing the footholds
In this dismal dark but the Angel.

She that waits for clinging death
to take departure into the unknown.
Showed me the tread
The whitewashed elm twisted with unseasoning,
Lest I stumble to trip and hurt myself.

The guardian was there
Ready for struggle to heave my body
from rest and out upon the plains
Where my body could only make the pledge
to be somebody.

I saw her radiant smile though she was not there, yet
In the vision I saw the young Athenea
And her wantonness stirred me into work
and taking on a new Arthurian folly.

When the grape was too young to drink
Upholding the fruit, golden with
burnt sienna to throw it into the vat
Was all the worth that my energy could
giving knowing
That the fruit of the vine would be for prosperity.

Nothing save for the fumble of a
lost sleepless bird in a hedgerow
On this troubled sleepless night.
When tiredness is lost through tiredness
And the dew, that honeyed dew
Lingers listfully longing for the dawn
and this still heat to bake the day and scorch the lowland grasses.
And the day that hot summers day
with the heath steeped in violet heathered hazes.

The heat of this summer's day was lazy,
    and still.
One could only hear the bubbling
    restlessly in the ear, and to follow.
 My ego led me to this resting place.
Floods of tears and then to remember
Under this shade of an apple
With its fruit
Dripping around my lips in its first bite
Was to remember and be thankful
For this space that gave me counsel.

The ground was parched and broken.
Fine grainy lines liken to an old man
That I was treading on, on the peat,
stretched blackened, and brown.
Edged with lines of exhausted grey clay
I walked out into this summer's day
With little giving of this slow air
To sustain the life within me save for this moment
When hearts are united and tomorrow
holds no problems.

The Black bridge waited and
welcomed me.
Iron-railed she stretched her man-
made splendour horizontally yet of an
abstract nature
To be here was to be part of and I
found little to contrast this structure to
the lowland landscape.
Clothed in handsome ivy green and stringy,
And decked with other fineries,

lichen yellowed and mellowed with
maturity,
The concrete moulded blockwork stood
proud, forlorn,
awaiting the tackle box with its plastic thud
And tinkling of tackle unseen to
the restless yet eager eye.

Beauty! — What a lucky man I am
To have fate lend me your love and promises!
　　　　— and further more
Look at this world that you and I
have yet to re-model and fashion in our likeness.
To feel you near is all I ask,
The rest is yours and welcomed.
She passed a glance, knowing
She was too good to share my immaturity.
Ascending up into
heaven she turned around and
Smiled at the boy in me
Playing with the ground.

Heaven sent the mud and this peat land,
Gave the water an earthly smell,
Homeliness, the nectar that my
baseness called upon to be whole.
Coupled by the draping marsh willow-herbs
Purpled and pale just
following the treads my weary feet pursuing?
And,
Should I take up pollen, rich and almost spoonful,
To sneeze is just a reminder that
Chance has allowed me to do so.

When eels wriggle blindly,
In the thick slimy silt
Of a wetland that
is paceless,
Waiting fast feet and restlessness.

A lovely day hazed with troubled
pollen disturbed from their flowers,
A pleasant day to sit by the bank
And spend social hours with the
golden lady that gave a new day.

She was near, she was at hand
Her gaze was directed but she allowed me
To follow the unknown
In search of my answers.
I likened her to my mother
Maternal and with an open ear
The listener to my heart and head's
desires.

Burnish the clouds
Make them shine silvery grey and
tell me it isn't so
That you have to go, and leave me not
Your footprints and me alone standing
in this virgin snow.
Oh the skate ring over this land
listening to the groaning crack that
followed my play
You were near, very near guiding me
the way.

Chastised by the purity of the Angel fair

Who called my name softly
From this wilderness wake
When the redwing seems worried with flight
Not knowing the season she wings for
Or the scurry of the Nuthatch shows
Uncertainty for the next hollow to inspect
For fruits within the apple tree,
I sat slowly down
With an empty head awaiting
Her guidance and inspiration.

Her gown flowed old with trailing whispers
Of homespun linen cobwebbed fine they touched down to the peat,
waiting for a Vatican frame
So others could view her openness and pay for worship.
My mind cast glances of failing
cycles, turning and reeling on the
spinning frame
That she was treading with an
open shoe showing small pale toes
Deprived of blood through labour,
Yet eager to clothe my body with a garment
new for the next exchange of thoughts.

My father died here for his eternal
glory
So that others would follow and
eventually forget him in their drunken
pub talk yet,
My dad took the chance to befriend
the lady
And she by chance took him away.

To compose let us let this fable dance

With merry footsteps
And take the too steeped
To two-step dance upon this hill.

The graze was old —,
Dry with dark bloodied scab it itched for
Scratching and I scratched the itch away
To make the wound young again.
Bleeding in oozing spots I'll rub them
fresh into skin and think of how or when
it happened?

To awake on this morning one is only aware
Of warm sheets, because the evening night
was too hot for blanket or duvet
And a body smelling
In want of warm bath with its water
soothing
And cleansing the exteriors whilst the
awaiting
Scrubs the dirt from within me.

The day broke long time
Before I awoke with a wilderness in my mouth,
The parched barren plain
Nicotined brown through abuse
Cried out for water and the bright work chromium of man
Flowed out a sparkling oasis
Rippling around the basin ring
Out flowing away
My thirst remaining seeking
The hop again or perhaps a coffee blackened
and hot to make the engine warm

So it could fire and perform again.

Cow parsley adorned the
wayside crowned with
white pungent smelling
flowers, pancaked spread
through the wild rose
And blackberry orphaned
in the hedgerow
By its unsociable thorn
Wandering, soiled by flies
the fruits drifted through the elm
And proud, biting nettle.

She couldn't go,
Her gaze told me so that certain stare
across this legless table spread out over this moor
Covering each hollow and rhine
With the very cloth that she was clothed in
That Nakedness was mine but to be shared
And the choice was hers and hard
How could I take away the lady with
a hand outstretched to the maternal child
Wanting to travel and
Having to leave for adventures new.
To leave her bosom and its rich sweet milk
To return eventually a man
With a redeeming heart,
aged face and social scars and
a head of grey hair
to rest upon the clay.

The legs draped like washed linen,

Sagging heavy with use and abuse
I turned to look,
And nothing,
Nothing in me aroused the boy and I forgot her smell.
Likened to an old barn, seasoned with age,
And lost active air I turned to sleep
And in rest —
I waited for her warm unseasoness, —
That fragrance that gave my soul the wholeness
Of being a man in a biting world.

A grey day I could see —,
Clouds of sorrow billowing in their own wake
The fields lie dead save for the graze
That my kitten gave, festering young in an
older yet ungiving skin in an unburnt hand
And the blackbird cried alone
In her scurry to aware ourselves,
Of the torment yet to happen;
A shrill cry and then another
And then the cloud gave way to her
aching load and
let loose her burden upon the moor.
Again and again in dousing sprays
and with violence,
The storm gashed the man within me,
and a boy was born to allow
himself to stand in the rain.

In this scene
Stippled by low Mendip cloud
And the panting stench of hot
breathless horses

Dragging the iron plough and its sharp
tooth biting the turf
Turning the furrow making for the change
For the unborn seedling
Smothering the weed with soil
Tram-lined across the field
They dragged the wheel-less load
To the swishing tails and the
timeless crack
      of the Master's whip.
And further out
Young children and their mothers
Crouched and cradled
Armfuls of sticks to bind and
Knot with hairy twine
Nestled warm and dry beneath the
peat to light on those looming chilly
evenings in the home.
Where fathers sit straddled in leather
gaiters warming hands and bodies with mulled spicy cider and
conversation.

The Withys have changed colour
and are ripe for the
flat capped gentlemen
To take the sickle upon them
And cut them in ranks
Built in teepee shaped cones
to dry for the dry store when men
Whistle John Barleycorn again
And uncomplainingly cough in the mustiness.

The dew dared not go

In event of reprisals from the lady,
She stood erect in her modesty
Then a knowing wave
To the birds that fluttered high
As she walked
Leaving mist arousing in her foot path.
Eternal spirit!
Why leave the tread to follow
For one so uncertain as I?
"Parceval" she whispered
"Follow me and leave your armour
Rusting through misuse
For the scrap man to clear now
this railway is gone and I
will lead you to the fruits."

The Messenger   September 1978

I lay in semi-slumber
Listening to the lullabies of the evening wind.
She has a tune for the daylight hours
But it's always the night songs,
That play in my head.
      A whirling wind,
That taps the window pane,
And whispers in the cracks sweet messages,
Of ageless love and promises,
That I'll keep in my heart for you.
      My shapeless messenger
That turns up Autumn leaves
Writes upon them sweet tunes
Then sends them weaving waving over hedgerows,
And far into the sky.
Tossed like golden curls
She lays them on the dunes.
I watch the curtain wave a last Goodbye,
And who knows the meaning of these letters?.
Only you and I......

Grub

Grub said she'd been waiting all day for her dad's
return and also for her mum
She said she looked up to the sky
And she saw an aeroplane go by
and waved in case it was her mum's plane
But no-one waved back and we are by ourselves again.

Watch it Grow   August 1977

Let there be two cities,
Yours and mine,
But one day, when our love's battles won, —
Let them converge,
And grow into one.....

My walls are of sand,
Under your touch
They crumble away into Nothing, —
Less than dust in the wind.
Astirred in time as you.

My rooms are all strong,
The land I stand on smites for a love —
In yearning,
That maketh me lost
Yet yearning your flesh can sustain me.....

My windows so glazed
Bedimming the light that emits an auxiliary Force,
Glowing so strong
No shadows are cast,
Until the Flame,
Burns me at Last —
To you I bequeath my Ash.....

My love babbles still,
From people deep within me
For love is all around me
for I AM, the city.....

How Do You Sleep? August 1977

Who now stirs the embers of your fire,
To place another log?
Who holds your tender hand
To lead you through the fog,
And, every night he prays your soul to keep,
Tell me my lovely,

How do you sleep?

Who now holds you tight and calls aloud
Your name,
And talks to you each night,
About his claim to fame?
Who now throws the clothes down in a tangled heap?
Tell me my lovely, —

How do you sleep?

Who adorns your head with posies,
Are you sure that they're not thorns?
Impales you on the cross,
Between his very horns,

Is he the wolf,
That counts the shepherd's sheep?
Pray, tell me my lovely, —

How do you sleep?

Who now jokes with you to ease a heavy heart,
And tells that you two
Should never be apart?
I hear that every night
He entertains the street,
Tell me my lovely, —

How do you sleep?

Who now lives a life alone,
Slowly works away?
The one that you deserve,
Enlightens every day.

Is he the shepherd,
That looks upon the sheep?
Tell me my lovely, —

How do you sleep?

Who but I can tell you,
That in this life of sin,
Not only there's a start,
But also there's an end?
And love becomes a habit
Rather than a feeling Deep —

So tell me my lovely,

"How can you sleep?"

An Angel Came Walking   1993

Lifeless sat I amid the
            sacred garden
And stillness was the pond now
            so shallow
In the summer heat.
Radiance turning Golden and for
            a short while
I felt no longer alone in my own space.
And for the company of her smile —,
An observer blind could cast an eye to see
            me alone talking.
But to the wise, they smiled too —, knowing
            the angel was with me
                    and together we
                    were walking

My Beloved Tree   August 1977

Yes, in some procumbented manner,
We once watched the last fading minutes,
Of today
Through the branches
Of this tree.
Sapped dry of colour,
The disease was strong,
To pierce within thee too.

And as you dry and die,
So shall my love die.

Prominent roots that once embedded my body,
From shade or storm.
Can now only hide my face from scorn
And,
Staring o'er fields of yellow,
You silhouette still blocks my sun,
The image that I so dearly loved

Upon the cart looks so forlorn,
I sit back helpless,
Watching skylarks cry above the corn.

Big City Lights   Jan 9th 1974

Look at the ladies,
In the streets.
They are all unhappy,
But they do not weep.
The ones that laugh
Eat from empty plates.
Those that just stare
Are aware,
of their fate.
As they bypass this world,
With Its Big City Lights.
They dream of their likes,
And dislikes.
As they spin a long web,
Of hope and peace.
The world keeps on spinning —
Will it ever cease?

Look at their children,
Long-faced and lean.
Faced full of spite.
Their hearts so mean,
They beg from the Gutters
And steal off the Roads, —
Just think of the future
And what it beholds.
Some feel that freedom,
And their feelings untwine,
But they normally do wrong
And walk down the line.

Each face is different,
Each body too.
Just underfed people the old
And the new.
Eyes that have sunken,
Worn cheekbones cold grey,
The Crowd just squirm by
With nothing to say.

Look at the houses,
With Black City walls
Hang all like dominoes,
Until one falls.
Windows so small,
No sunlight goes through,
A baby was crying,
Yet no-one knew.
Only the blackhouse,
And long smoke clouds
That mourn for the dead
Though no prayer is said.

Look at the worker,
Unshaven and old.
Been out all day,
Builds one more new road.
Look in his eyes, and
What do you see?
Nothing's inside but,
Pictures of me.
Each eyes mirror reflects
All it sees.
Each limb s filthy,

Arms, legs and knees.
Your feet are bare,
your clothes so torn,
His face looks skyward —
"Why was I born?"

Look into the darkness,
And try to look through,
And think of the city
Can this really —
       Be you?

The Fall   June 1998

Lost summers,
Spilt wine and twilight time,
Cold Comfort Farm flickering on the cornered TV,
Cosy-rosy wintered toes those
Cold winter evenings
Then summer days
Were times we'd look forward to.
No more arguments
Children squabbling
Children and tender loving touches
No more cat fights
And crockery breakages
No more swallows
Not even a lone one in a purpled crazy sky
No more sunlit summers.

Somerset   1978

"I have a love for Somerset....."

The Sedgemoor drain
Pours out her earthly stills.
— Close guarded by fishermen.
Whilst,
On the skyline,
Tall, grey undaunting shapes,
Of dying Elms
        Stippled by low clouds —
        Surround the Mendip Hills.......

Those wind-sketched roaming hills,
Reach out for wondering hands.
You'll stumble o'er footways,
That lead you to the sands.
Bleating sheep will comfort you —
        and guide you all the way.......

Oh! deep rich swirling mists,
That hide the painted fields;
That cover up the primrose,
Awake the daffodils!
And wildlife rise up from slumber
For in these early hours
        the trees just hide their colours.......

On Return from the Gulf   1991

Your mother need not cry
Standing solitary in the mourning crowd
to cast her eyes
and her squatted body upwards
So that she can look up to see the Son
That shines for her every morning
He will not come but wait! —,
He'll wait for her in a warmer place
Asleep in the sand
And his body she'll remember well,
Chastised by his own innocence.
As the boat comes in she'll wait by the
          rotting quay
Watching the joy and sorrow
Watching the seagulls flee
And waiting for the boat to return again
Waiting for her reddened eyes
To be freed from pain........

The Magi 1977

3 Kings came to see this man
3 Kings came to watch and stand
3 Shepherds came to share and smiled
3 poor men to see the child.
One kind came with folded robes
One King came to see his fold
One Kind held a lamb so small
And 3 Kings came that were so poor.
One King came with shepherd's crook
One King came with learned book
One King came with frankincense
One King came with common sense
One King brought a crock of gold
One King gave his love to hold
One King gave a gift of myrrh.
And 3 wise men saw a baby fair.

Poverty   1971

Yes,
I know what poverty is.
To gnaw gnawed bones from Last Sunday's dinner,
To sleep between worn linens,
And feel the cold of winter and the cold minds of the
Faceless rich men.
The cat is hungry,
Who isn't?

In this blinded confusion our minds tick over and cry
For our God's mercy.
You never know how a poor man feels until you,
Have starved yourself.

Hunger isn't known to the rich,
But to the poor man it's just another daily event.
Golf, sailing, NIGHTCLUBS?
Gambling,
          and you're talking.

Begged, stole or lent
I've seen men grovel until those cool clean greenies
Are Spent.

The cheapest drinks expensive,
The cheapest food is bread,
God make us truly thankful and keep us clean in
MIND so that our HEADS will not REEK as the clothes
on our BODIES or the skin on our BACKS which bear the
Impurities of the world and weigh us down...........

I sometimes cry alone,
My whispering prayers matter none to the rich man nor do
Those tears that wet the soil that I walk.
My home, small little,
Squalid where woodlice, cockroach, and earwigs refuse to
Live;
Lies silent and waits for my return.
Down unlit roads I roam, to find what I can pawn.
Each night I sleep alone,
And wait until the Dawn...........

Now I Know   1st Oct 1977

You may have eased
My sleep,
When I was troubled,
But now to know
And look at you,
My hardships doubled....

To seek for someone else,
How long can this last,
For sorrow,
Breeds more sorrow,
From such a fearful task....

I wish it only true,
That only you
I knew.....

Still the Problem Lingers   1976 - 1977

Still the evening tide,
Was breaking,
On a shore where nothing's waking,
In a time that I once knew.

In my mind,
A door is open,
Where a man can show his feelings,
Of a life that lies in hand.

Oh yes, to me it's just a dream,
Where a man can show he's free,
And talk,
Just like the sea.

In the twilight stands a door,
To the paths that go so far,
But to me it's
just
        Ajar....

The Philosophy of Love   17 Feb '82

As Seen Through the Eyes of an Old Man

An Old man grey and withered with age, and famed for knowing the strangest secrets of life lived alone on top of a high mountain where his only companions were the sun and the sky.

He wasn't as aged as the mountain he so clearly loved or of the ribbons of sparkling rivers so far below him yet he knew of their origin, source and of the people that succumbed to their needs.

It so happened one vacant day that in his silent gaze he was surprised to see a young boy struggling with great effort to reach him. He could see the boy was plagued with a trouble for his face had a look of curiosity deep set in his eyes that their sparkle was a glaze of questioning. The boy although tired and in need of comfort sat down exhausted at a safe distance from the man's feet as he was aware that strangers sometimes may be angered by visitors.

"Take rest boy and let your breath be regained. Then, when you're ready, tell me why you have made such a journey to see me."

"I seek a truth" said the boy "that will reassure my heart for I am soon to take a wife of whom I dearly love. I have thought of love but in the world of men and their deceit I have lost its values in riddles that now worry me. The world has lost its heart and now bleeds for a new kind of understanding."

This made the old man laugh so much that tears were seen to brim his eyes.

"My life I have chosen to live alone for I too was once like you and the question you wish me to answer is the only one I cannot for I myself am still seeking."

But fear not for I know of some of these values.

And as he spake he changed his emotion so great that it was seen that the clouds did clear and the air crackled with renewed freshness.

"In love you can share a conversation
That needs no uttered words
And know that silence is no longer a word fit for
solitude but only a moment when your hearts are
completely united,
As with that droozy sleep that closes each day,
You can watch her in your dreams.
I have held those material things
That man so dearly loves —
Silver and Gold too!!
And stones of many precious shapes and colours.
I have heard of music that flows
So sweet from the lips of the chosen —,
But in life so far —,
I have never valued anything more great
Than the power of understanding others.
If you can stand by a shore,
Neath a golden sky and reach out your hand
to feel hers near,
You will know that she will always be there —,
To raise your kindled spirit
As the Autumn wind does stir dead leaves.
For now becomes a time
When even troubles become shared things —,
And at the end of a long and fruit filled life.
Should death chance to dash its fatal blow,
If you can lie in a place so soft and warm,
And feel her hand soothing away the fear
At least you will know you have lived and loved,
And on closing those tiring eyes,
Say nothing more than 'I AM A MAN!'"

The Chaos of Design   12/6/91

The effect of designing is to initiate change in all man-made things, taking obviously into account the conscious or subconscious influence of the natural world and social change. The fundamental importance, above all, in the concept of design as a pure subject is rationality therefore the design process above all else is one of rational logical analysis. This is emphasised strongly by my philosophy that all design represents a fundamental and rigorous activity where young people are enriched and follow through a planned sequence of steps and cycles until he or she recognises the best of all possible solutions.

I say reluctantly that, The Bauhaus is dead in today's design school based activity — what a shame when we are having to nurture uncertainties in a vague combination of tradition, expediency and chance. Design is now living in a unilateral past where the requirements of today's 'A' Levels predominate and monopolise the specification. I now unfortunately impose my considerations of skill upon the availability of the materials to my disposal and in doing so await the revival of my respected learnings.

How can I alone impose technological requirements as I have a client who is acting adversely to impose his considerations and lacking the skill and knowledge with his directives?

May I commend today's teachers of any design activity by saying to you all that you are brilliantly successful but only incompletely are you rational. I wish to change all this but am only a sad case (to quote James Joyce) waiting on a railway track to let the train cut off my voice.

The Inebriate Taunton Man   12 Aug 1977

40 hours a day,
40 hours of pain,
When the money's game
The work still remains —
"Hey Mister! can you lend me a bob?"

Don't go near,
For he's a ragamuffin,
Don't you stare,
Even though he don't care,
People pass him on by
Looking down just roam,

Can't they see he hasn't got a home?!

Had a family,
Full grown family-tree,
But the tax man came on day,
And cut the roots away.
Relations looked around,
Walked him underground.
"Hey Mister! can you lend me a bob?"

I'll Tell another story,
If you wait a mo'.
But when this bottle's gone,
I'll just wander on — to the shops,
And fill the bugger up.

"Hey Mister! can you lend me a bob?"

I was a wealthy man,
I owned a lot of land.
Worked there all the time
But became an underline.
They squeezed me for more,
And now I just say,
          I drank it all away.

I've often walked this town,
Stumbled over ground,
In irregular paces
I've seen a lot of faces.
I've whistled at the dames,
I had a claim to fame,
"Hey Mister! can you lend me a bob?"

Cos,
I am often in the gutter,
Getting me clothes wet,
The people sometimes throw me lighted cigarette stubs,
I am in the rain,
Getting long, wet hair,
But people turn their heads —
          no longer care.

Into the Mirror   25/2/83

The day will come my friends
When you can gaze into a mirror and really see yourselves —
        — There is a journey through manhood
Where a man seeks his predetermined goal and that is
·The laboursome task of the search for his own identity.
He will start by borrowing one
In respect of an absent friend
And will model his ideas upon the words of the wise and famous.
In his work he will toil
And despair by criticism and unkind words.
He will strive to be himself
And learn the hidden knowledge of living with and loving others.
He will feel pain and sorrow
And a bitterness towards his world of ambition.
        — It is then that his spirit may die
And he will cast aside himself and follow instruction
Or he may battle on
Against all odds to stand straight
Although his back may be bent and his heart broken
And on return to a home
He can gaze into the mirror
And instead of admiring someone else —,
                He will only see himself.

The Farmer   October 1977

Last winter,
'Twas so cold,
The skin had cracked
All on his face so charactered,
The making of this man.
And hot spring days
Reached out for him to come,
To hold the Plough.

He toiled the soil,
With a back abent with work and age,
Making sweat streams into rivers,
That ran into the brook,
Where sleeping fishes dreamed for him,
On distant river beds.

The day grew hotter,
In the noon day sun,
And shadows hid from light
As swishing tails,
Of scorning dribbling cows,
Licked,
Sparkling salty block —
        and watched him.

He pushed and steered
The furrow,
Against another sod,
And horses strained their aching veins
Stumbling o'er the ground,

Whilst drunken bot flies,
Teased them on —
To start another Run.

This summer will be fruitful,
Over laden to the bough,
My wheat sheaves lie golden
Dormant in this ground .... ,
But,
Who knows,
Where my life goes?
Through fading Autumn Woodlands,
Amongst these twisted headlands,
I've lurched an aching body
To bend each fruitful bough,
Sought each seed,
And gave it life,
Revealed beneath the plough.

"What Beauty!" people say,
I've cracked the frozen screen,
And revealed another day.
Beneath
Encrusted snow
I've stayed here all the while,
I am good and rich and golden,

I am this Spring Soil.

I cut and scrape the ground,
To rust and heave my way,
Through stone, rock, mortar,
Peat or hardened clay,

To bed these seeds somehow,
I am an iron labourer,
Me ——,
          The Plough.

I see no need,
To cling to rock and fasten,
Small yet always fertile,
To everyone I feed,
Always at the tempest mercy,
Me ——,
          The Seed.

"I guide and love you all,
Stand bold in muddened armour,
I hold and love you all,
For I am the Farmer ...."
And man shall suffer on,
Until he gets turned on,
My bothers will flow on,
For I am one of many,
          And nature gives in Plenty.

My Invitation   2016

I remember Your table at the Cheap Hotel.
I'd arrived earlier sat in a corner Waiting.
Your dress looked good!
Your manner also but you didn't
Know I was there —
As if you should.
Punters came and people went,
backed away when they had spent.
You just picked up a menu
And by fingering those words —,
A poor reader or short-sighted.
To be obtuse —,
But what's the point of picking
Expensive meals of little use.
I sat smelling the room
Kitchen flavours and your cheap perfume
As those walls gathered in
I still sat in that corner within
The boundary of my thought,
Trying to work out your price
Of if you had already been bought.
May I like You? —,
After all you were invited.
That's the trouble with You —,
I get all excited
So I'll still sit here by and by
I failed to tell You — I was shy...

Watching the Gulls

Seagulls inland —,
The coastal winds
Have driven them in.
Driving as falling snow —,
They dip and bow.
Driven faces to the wind.
It was cold,
Some say snow had fallen —
and I saw its white shining back
Lying at rest on these Mendip Hills.
Dusting everything with softness
And silencing the daily noise
of distant tractors
bringing the milk in....
The wood was silent
Some trees were tired from the heavy snow
and leaned upon wooden hearted partners
Some lay down exhausted amongst the
bursting pine cones
That scattered and glistened upon the
icy ground.

It was cold —,
but somewhere in my heart
It was Christmas.
It tingles toes and bodies,
Sparkles up our children's faces.

Christmas you old dog I see you!
winking at me through the tinsel

In trimmings festooned in this lowly room
I see you smiling in the fire with a
cunning grin
Greeting all my people with a welcoming eye
Is it your message I hear in the wind
Or the faint lullaby of a
Wise King?
Whilst I, sit here with my eyes to this
open sky,
I hear you're born again —,
In a desperate bid to win old values
Come please cast your mantle down,
Enliven up this town!
Weigh down all the fir trees bough
The rusting snow capped ploughs.
But leave me here to think again
For today I stare,
Watching seagulls snowing
In this winter's air.

The Unexpected Realism   10 Aug 1977

Yet another candle reeled smoke around this Room,
Refulgent on wall and picture,
Amidst the fading gloom.

Another day toiled on.

Dipping yellow finger flames glow on, and on,
To cut my thoughts — of loneliness.

I've made many pictures from peeling plaster,
Of you —
> "Look see, here lies the face of Beauty!"
> that destroyed me.....

Dripping molten wax,
Shadowed ghosts flicked and dodged the room,
One more lonely letter,
The scent upon my shirt,
> Her very own perfume —
Or had it been a gift?
> From the prospective Groom.

Her mother said to me,
"I think you're wrong,
She's got a fi-anc-ee".

I bit my tongue to refrain:
"It's the pain that makes the day".
The moths only tell me,
That life revolves in circles like you've learnt,

But even moths get close I've seen their f
feet get burnt.

Maybe as I've stated,
To a loved one that I'd dated,
"I am just a new toy",
At first I am used,
Then Abused.
Treated like something she'd never saw,
But then I am thrown against the wall.....

It's only, lonely days of rain,
When I am in her arms again
"he's something new!"

"But I've got feelings too".....

In my void of painful heartbreaks,
I try to give a love that aches,

GOSSIPS, FEAR and CHILDNESS,
        cannot suffice my loneliness.

It's something grown within me,
Yes, but to you a man is something that,
"nature gives in plenty".

What more can I mention,
But ask my God for Redemption,
He's a learned man too,
I hopes he forgives us two.

But of all things most,

I pray he keeps me close,
  to you.

  *"Ab imo pectore"

* *From the bottom of my heart.*

For the One I Love   Oct 1977

"It feels like a seed,
That's almost,
Wind blown
To your garden where we can
Watch it grow.....
I hope you understand,
That love was never
Taught at school,
And now it's time for me,
To show you.....

Tears like dew upon
the grass,
Right down to the smallest one,
Only on my face alone,
Linger in the sun.....

You'll just get up,
Each day
But it's time to turn another page,
Of your life,

But don't burn the candle
At both ends,
Cos. one day they'll meet
And I'd hate to see,
The flame die.....

You're not just a girl,
To me, another world,
Where I can start
A new life,
And as each day,
That now passes,
Of all contempt I feel,
Is the torture of having to spend,
One less day
With you.....

It's time to ride again,
Around another corner of life —
You'll see a feast of golden shops,
Where you can feed your eyes,
I hope that you'll remember if you fail me,
That around another corner,
You're not short of
            Paradise.....

It's time to realise,
That love was never taught at school,
An unacquainted rule,
Just and just again,
I knew,
They could never show you.....

Love, as a flower that you see,
Wilts before your very eyes,
Give it warmth and kindness,
Never wait,
Until it dies.....

They'll paint your name,
In watercolours,
But to me you'll remain,
For I will never leave you,
In the rain.....

Never say 'No'
To love you fool,
I hope you'll never forget that
Love was never taught at school.

Go now cherish all you memories,
Go give the Widow's mite,
Give 'em all you've got
Even give your name
Cos to me I don't know why
        you'll remain
                the same.....

Hand to them
A helping hand,
They'll kiss you so with one wet lip,
The other they may surely spit,
And leave the laughs behind,
        For as they drink regretting it
        You taste but wine.....

look before you leap,
But let me take the first step,
I've tread the path before.
It's time to be so true,
Cos. love was never taught at school.

It's just as in the Garden,
Wrapped in winter overgrowth,
The soil now sterile,
Can show a future growth.....

You need someone to lead to,
This feeling lies within you,
So,
Even scream your name,
For beauty serves so very few,
And you could show them
all.....

Reach for me,
The sparrow feeding from your reaching hand,
And let him feed from you,
This knowledge that you have,
The cold and broken heart,
You could make good......

He'll puff his breast and
sing
          "One saviour Oh! for the SPRING!"

Miriam   1971

Miriam is all the good things.
She's the smile that greets the lonely;
She's the light that makes my dawn.
To me she is everything,
I am glad that she was born.

Being   1971

To be alone,
Is not living.
To be afraid,
Is not thinking.
To be happy,
Is a dream.
To breath the air is nice,
They say it's good for your health.

Storm on a Hot Day   1971

Rain beats across the
World,
Water swirled,
Beneath the sky I cried out loud,
And cursed at the blackened cloud.
      Panic on the sand,
      Obeyed command.

The Craftsman   1971

I once knew a man
Who was worthy of his master,
He could shave with a plane,
Carve out of plaster
He was a craftsman
I one knew.
See him sanding a chair
Or making a table,
There was no craft that
He wasn't able.
He was a magician
Stood by a fire
With sparks into the air
He'd turn a tree,
      Into a chair.

Loneliness of a Tramp   1971

Night unfolds her cloak of tears,
Darkness haunts the ground;
Silence comes to comfort me upon the sun-parched mound.
Peace lies beside me,
Under tall shaded pines,
Moonlight floats on down, mingles with the misted ground.

Nature lies beside me under tall swaying pines,
Loneliness abides with me,
And slowly bends my mind.

As an encaged bird,
I cried for a friend;
My voice never ending,
Thoughts still remaining.

An unknown soul waiting for rest in a world that's never resting.
A man who keeps on walking,
And never finds his goal.

Tomorrow I think I will roam,
I don't know where.

I wish I had a home.

The Death of Love   April/May 1977

Let my mind write limbs within thy womb,
For I cannot part —,
From your frozen heart.

I immortalised the life you lead,
And so was crucified,
So that you —,
          could live.

Let my mind speak limbs within thy womb,
I hear they echo soft,
within thy tomb,
And tears of watered jewels like snail trails ran,
Across your stone-still cheeks,
          where first
Smiles began.
As tears of stalactites,
          Deep within thy eyes
          Took near,
          10,000 year to come.

The Feeling of Love (Pts 1&2*)   April/May 1977

Part One
Of all the contempt I feel,
That as each day that passes,
means one less day,
With you.
Those star-dust nights with him,
Deep in the heat I feel,
A pain that I deserve
For only you I serve.

Part Two
It may be wise to scorn
Such bitterness,
Yet two minds once loved each other,
To be humble,
I beseech you,
To let them try again.

By choosing her i was wrong,
For injustice pays my price for love.
Tis time that a loving heart
Cannot forget.

* NOTE:
In two parts, i.e.   Part A. Before - Looking at Heartbreak
*   Part B. After - Looking back at the Relationship.*

Dr Knew   by James Bond's Brother-in-Law

It wasn't an easy task. On that lonely deserted beach only distressed by the gull calling for a mate and the soft, calling whisper of the wind around the Pink Coral where the bacteria lay in the darkness bathed in a light lotion from seaweed extracts to avoid sunburn, that I took off my White Tuxedo. Removing the Silk tie that slid from around my neck like a loving girl's hand, I brushed my face with my palms. It was necessary because with no toiletries for many months - I had grown a beard. 'Where is Bond?' The voices said 'where is he with the perfect symmetry?'

The voices in my head said:

"Where is the smart Bond that the girls fancy? —
if you were a man you would take a razor and shave."
And truly I was unshaven, I was most unshaven.
A hollow drum had washed ashore
With lowly muffled haunting call,
As if a Church beyond the Hills
Rang out the Mourning Bells.

On the skyline burnt with the frying heat of a West Indian Sun, the grey hulk of my Submarine when down into the dark bowels of this sacred Ocean and was gone. The seething turbulent foam bubbled in a frenzy. Feeding time for the Sharks — The sailors had forgotten to close the hatch.

The boat had gone. I remember her gratitude when aboard and the Rum, shaken but not stirred and I paused, as often when I am not sure if this story will work, and wondered where was Martha?

We had both been assigned to investigate Beachcombing on a stretch of coastline that was a Site of Scientific Interest. The Ministry back at Whitehall, London, had Chosen Martha and my style for this mission. Me because I am smart and an Officer with infinite knowledge of the Migration of Periwinkles that I'd studied in North Somerset due to an overwhelming ache of Boredom and Martha? —

She knew nothing. Somewhere in her distant Blonde ancestry the bright genes had degenerated into a more powerful force - Beauty. She would accompany me on this dangerous adventure and when I've a moment or two to work out things I can sit her in front of me — and stare...

I'll make plans for her after the work is done. Take her out on the town. We'll catch the bus to a cheap Chelsea Hotel and I'll play Leonard Cohen songs at midnight for her on my Jew's Harp.

A packet of crisps, a can of Coke and clean underwear should do the trick. (I do hope she brings neither).

"Martha? Martha!" I called.

My voice with the word perfect diction wasn't working today so knowing she was Swedish I call again in French:

"Martha? Martha!"

" Qu'est-ce que c'est?" a voice replied.

I knew my broken Continental accent would provide clearer definition.

"I am over here lovely, jaw-dropper" I replied.

"Où êtes-vous?" said Martha with a voice that reminded me of what heaven could be like or the night when the Gendarmes arrested me for Kerb crawling when I couldn't find a place to park my Aston Martin.

"I'll go anywhere with you my favourite Martini Trifle Kiss Kiss" I said with my masterly vocabulary.

"I've found a big white curly shell in the sea but it's empty" said Martha, her lips swollen and rich like fruit at the hour of perfection.

"It's empty is it?"

"Yes, it's very hollow. It's been Nat King Coled" she said.

"Then it's dead," I replied.

"No — it is Not, if I press it to my ear I can hear his music. Oh, — hang on! If I turn my head a little I can get Glastonbury FM."

"Apart from turning me on so that I can't stand up to show you've aroused me, can you turn that shell off now as we've work to do."

She came around the rock face. Bathed in Celestial Light. Her blonde hair flowing as gossamer on a bird's wing then with a gentle gesture cast the shell back into the waters. Brushing soft white sand from her hands she proceeded to enter her find on the A4 tally chart that she'd made earlier with wax crayons.

"Which box do I tick?" she enquired.

"Pick any my sweetest Nectar only reserved for the Gods"

"Ummm. One potato, two potatoes, three potatoes o.u.t. spells out" and then the crayon snapped. The sharp impact brought back the nights when I was imprisoned in Cambodia and force-fed dry Jacob's Cream Crackers. They didn't break me, no sir, I didn't tell the Secrets of Shell-pickers. My mouth was full.

"Look here Martha! In this rock-pool. Something is moving."

She leaned over and I felt dizzy. The blood that had rushed to my nether regions had deprived my brain and I had to lie down.

"Why are you lying down?"

"To get a closer look at my sticky Toffee Apple only reserved for Fair-goers who have sixpence to spend," I said regaining my senses.

"It's a slug with a hard shell and eight legs and two eyes that stare at me," she said.

"I don't blame it."

"What is it? Is it foreign?"

"Ask it a question as recommended by the guidelines."

"Are you foreign?"

No reply.

"That's clearly told me from this Ladybird book of the Seaside that it's a Rare Mute Crab."

Having discarded the broken yellow crayon she reluctantly chose her second favourite colour and entered the find under the title 'Bad

Natured Things'.

The heat of the day got hotter and hotter. A blue haze came down over the sea and Martha looked deep into my parched eyes.

"Are you hot?"

I began to get a funny feeling that this blonde wasn't so daft after all.

"No, not at all my darling buds of May more beautiful than Pop Larkin," then turned to look at our findings neatly folded in a pretend fag-packet that 'Q' had engineered back in the Lab.

"Why is it in that Packet?" said the Shaft of Sunlit beauty more radiant than my electric fire back in Harlow.

"People don't smoke anymore. It's banned in most places and to the best of my understanding, if you drop a fag-butt on the streets of Bath all hell breaks loose! Spies aren't interested in smoking my drop-dead blonde who I want to snog" said I.

"What's a snog?" said the girl that melts my skin quicker than this heat.

"Here —, let me show You...."

to be Cont'd......

Getting Started 2016

It was a dark night. A cold, dark, damp night and the air was still like your quiet breathing. The morning sounds lay asleep waiting for alarm bells that gave this neighbourhood a meaning to live. What little hope on offer was locked away in a long paper coffer and then the cough started - and the dog barked. The start was always like this. Always the same cycle as the clockwise turn of spoons in dusty teacups. When mothers and fathers summoned awake their offspring to sleepishly go about their thing. Their pattern of order that always finished with the recurring problem of the tying of shoelace, the parting of hair against the kitchen mirror and then the sad departing from comfort into a rowdy schoolroom.

Father tapped his pipe against an open hand, returned it to an open mouth to blow a silent tune. The dog barked again then Mother helped it into the backyard with her boot. Father coughed again from a dry throat. Trying to clear an unblocked tube that only reminded him of the dust journey inside the factory.

When the lamplights turned their shining faces off and the sun started to grin a wry smile across the village, the community started to stir almost as mechanical in their motions as the minute hand upon the church clock that was always there. Always there to haunt thoughts that one day, one day it would be their time to be carried within the oaken doors.

Mother wiped her hands with the dishcloth then draped it like a grey shroud over the Cold tap. The Hot tap was special. It was rarely used except on Wednesday evenings when it was bath night. The day when the 'Rayburn' remained on all day to ensure the tank stayed hot or else some other temper temperature would switch on. The soft kiss on cheek and father held his strap of hessian which contained the sack that contained his lunch. Some dry biscuit from a dormant granny's recipe and a vacuum flask of brown, aging tea as old as the tree in the garden. In this village everything is recycled - even the tea leaves that would eventually be spread with an open hand over the compost heap by little Jenny. The small infant crawling on all fours because she loved to play in the garden with its barbed-wire boundary. Given time little Jenny would learn in her own way not to eat the tea-leaves, the compost or the little pale green wriggly things that live under cabbage leaves. Green curly leaves wrinkled like her father's working hands. Today though was bliss. The sun was up and the birds were singing just for her. Everything abounds and has a beauty even to the Common Enemy who somewhere also has loving parents....

Girl with Dog   2016

She was leaning on the wooden rail and looking out at the flood plain. The rushes whispered her beauty — but she was lovelier than the Day. So calm lay the blackened peat-encrusted waters. She was leaning on the wooden rail that dared not raise even a splinter to her soft, untouched skin. It was then that I chanced to see her. Stumbling up with my plastic bag I could not fail to notice such a radiant beauty bathing by the Floodgate in rippling warm light.

Was it a sigh that my senses called to me? No, surely no. I stand only a worker with hope in hand and torment swimming in my head.

The freshly cut grass reminded me of my place as I walked the tarmac path to my unlit door and I thought about her. She turned to muse at me - as only thinkers do then turned back to wonder at this World and the spaces between us and them.

"Such a beauty, I wish she was mine." I said but came to terms that I could barely feed myself - let alone a Golden Retriever.

In the Days of the Prophet 2016

To grow and become abundant all seeds need time and pressure. Men are much the same. They don't need water. They can't swim.
Bert the artisan thought he'd be an artist, make beautiful stained-glass windows in Wells Cathedral and other sacred places. His son thought the same. One of them got it right.

On a makeshift platform Bert felt good in himself. He liked high places. It gave him the notion that he was closer to God and in a funny way he performed God's work. He made windows that told stories, cut the coloured glass and elongated the limbs of the prophets so that people could see the pictures more clearly.

Son of Bert cut fingers and because he didn't know any stories of anybody, even prophets, he just jumbled the pieces together and called it Modern Art. Son of Bert couldn't read. Son of Bert wasn't too good at Stained-glass either. He just grew up and grew older and wondered in awe - at his father's work.

John   2016

Old John is dead.
'Gone on' they said.
That Bogie Man really was there.
Not under his bed —,
But his favourite Chair.
A special seat
A daughter's treat.
For his old age birthday Party.
The day he ate too much broth
From a plastic straw
And go all kinds of Farty.

Old John is gone,
'He's wandered on'
That disease had made him do it.
No idea about the price of Bread
'Was it really £500' I heard him say
'No it's a thousand'
His loving daughter said.

Old John's moved on
He's dead and gone
Walked out to take the Air.
He didn't see that Bogie Man
So tripped and fell the stair.

Marriage Bliss

Yes,
      I lived with Her,
She was the driving force behind
My depression.
And always in my side.
In this life I thought:
"If only I could live for the moment!"
But she even kept that locked away.
Wanted that new dress
Wanted me to hire young Mayble
To tidy the mess
Wanted.....,
Wanted.....,
Wanted...

And then I saw her advert in the Paper.
It had a picture of Bill Gates on it
And said...
Wanted.

Prelude for the Morning   2016

John sat at the Breakfast table staring at the vapour rising from a steaming cup of coffee.

The cup stared back at him. The surface transfer of a black cat stuck to the grimy surface always stared at him so John turned the cup because he didn't really like cats.

The toast lay organised as if to remind him of a patio that needed laying. John wasn't too bothered. He didn't have a patio. He lived in a high-rise flat and thought of better uses for large heavy slabs like dropping them from his balcony to squash the swarm littering the streets.

The radio was on. He wondered why? He couldn't remember switching it on. Was it last Sunday? The radio told him to stay indoors because the weather was going to be frightening. "Weather never scares me," said John, "Only loud bangs!"

There was a loud bang outside. The Wheelie-Bin men had arrived. John thought had he put his rubbish out? Then John thought about another use for patio slabs.

Amid the faint layer of breadcrumbs that irritated his skin sat a large jar of thick cut Marmalade. It oozed over the rim slowly like a great big orange slug. John looked at it glistening in the lamplight. Why did he buy it? He didn't like marmalade. He did like slugs though especially orange ones so he lay a piece of toast over it knowing that orange slugs aren't too clever so might think that the toast was a nice flat rock to hide under.

Across the room hung a picture of a beautiful girl in a bathing costume its colour faded by the constant bathing of strong sunlight over the years. It was Margery! Margery with the bathing cap that made her look prematurely bald. John remembered taking that picture with his throw-away camera that cost him a few quid. He even remembered that day when he bought her candy floss and a 99 ice-cream and she was sick in the overbearing heat of a public bus on the way home. It didn't bother him at all as he had paper tissues to assist in cleaning her up. He remembered her lovely face looking at him as if he was a stranger she'd never met.

John loved that day so he framed the photo and hung it there in a special place.

John loved the day at Butlin's with the swingy swing-boats and the ducks with the green shit they made and he never ate spinach after that. He loved the cry of the sea-gulls. He loved the salt-sea air in his nose. He loved Margery. Margery didn't love him. She thought he was as odd as a box of frogs.

The Passage   2016

It is with the utmost respect that I have to inform you of the sad passing of my dearest Housemate. It was expected but there was always hope that he would have carried on a little longer, after all, he was always strong in body and although not a Churchgoer - we seemed to respect his manner in all kinds of ways.

Last Saturday he complained of a change within his feeble frame. I ignored him. He usually grumbled about something, even the weather! Why, if it was hot he couldn't wear a winter coat or if it was freezing that he didn't fancy swimming down by the river.

The Death Certificate confirmed that he was definitely dead. Snuffed it without even leaving a note or some kind of Will. I haven't a clue what will become of his stockpile of work or even his collections of framed documents written in Indian Ink upon the finest vellum. Some of which dates back centuries. He will be missed dearly by his family as they came and gathered by the front door to see him off.

I gently eased his body out of the building with a soft Camelhaired brush that I usually reserve only for my finest paintings.

The Oldest Silverfish in the house had died and all that was left behind was a faint dusty smudge on the Persian Rug where his body had been discovered after I had stepped on him.

1960's Disco Memory   2016

I danced in my own sweat.
As wet as the girl's thighs
As I 'legged her' in the Disco.

Never did know,
What I'd do with that Hard-on
Maybe do some scouting
Make a Jamboree Tent
Lying flat in Bed. — or,

A Flagpost in the Garden
Like all things that die
Standing half-mast in the Morning
It's flagging as all things Go.
Until the heated, sweaty atmosphere —,
Of Saturday Disco.

The Wait   2016

I will wait for You
There is nothing else to do.
A memory still haunts me of how we
became and what you see in me.
A flash of light on a Kingfisher's Wing,
And then you were gone again with your thing.
They say Sweden —,
But it's too far to walk and,
The Policeman took my car and all —
They said it'll be raffled as a Prize
At their Annual Policeman's Ball.
I hadn't really been drinking,
I was too busy in my head —
            thinking.
Of You and maybe getting
Some swimming lessons
Or even better
Maybe buying one of those aeroplane flights
That I've heard of and read
In a newsletter.
Between us lies a Great Open Sea
That what stops us
From being You and Me....

I'll wait for You,
There is nothing else to do....

Funeral Rights   2016

"Who are these people and why are they here? I don't know them and you've left it a bit late to book an appointment. I suppose you're just being nosey and turned up to see who else is being nosey. Are you all satisfied now?

There's a few .I recognise over there. They didn't find the time though to recognise me when I needed a quid. Funny how we all seem to make some excuse. That you didn't know. That you were unaware. i was fully aware and I'll remember you for the help or food and shelter that never appeared.

You all became aware when my name changed and I transformed into a better person. You even said good things about me and things that went like "I knew he could do it!" i did, by myself. Who are you? I don't know you. Have we met?

I am so glad that I can't talk to you all today, so glad... but, I think you'll all know what I'll say.

So, without anymore fuss I've chosen a hymn that you'll all never know. It's in Swedish!

Now - Get on with it!

Amen.

Glastonbury Pipe Dreams   2016

Please don't Wake us from our Dreams,
Life around here isn't all it Seems —,
Here! Have one of these Baby Moonbeams.
        Who on Earth last night was bawling?
The phones ringing - my doctor's Calling.

"Have you seen my latest Tablet?"
I don't need one —, I've a bag full.
"Fisherman's Friend?"
Guess you can it that — "Ahem....."

Running around like a Blue-Ass-Fly,
On these crazy Rainy Afternoons.
Must have been something spiked,
In these Magic Mushrooms
That's almost like an Act of Treason!
I can't think now, of any Reason.

He's a Good Bloke,
Always handy for a Smoke.
I've given up buying expensive Fags,
I prefer your brand — "BLAGS."

The Job Centre interview went well they said.
Cost me four quid on the bus fares to Wells!
Now I am skint and out of bread.
I don't need yours — it smells.
Way past its Smell-by-Date
I've gotta see "Mike-the-Deal —"
        I am running late.

There's those men up by the Market Cross again,
I think they're off-duty policemen
There's those men in the suits selling
Redemption to the Innocent
Invitations to the House of God —
What's the breakfast like?
I hear
They give pork to the Synagogues
Coal from Newcastle
Baccie from Bristol —
By the way —,
If you want some,
            I've a Ship full!

What day of the week am I living in?
Have you any food to cook?
I had a bad dream last Night
It involved work.

Just Sit   2016

Nothing is so important,
That it cannot be done 'til tomorrow.
The Barber can wait another day
And so can supper.
I sit her in the Sun, —, the Upper -
Hand can be postponed today.
Leave my Obituary on the Backburner. God,
and I will sort it out
When we've the Time.....

Money for Nothing   2016

Henry said that the extra cash would come in handy. He wanted a new shed on his allotment. Way down on the edge of the moor stretched his earthen patch, Plot 42 - he admired Plot 43 which was next to his. It had an easier access to water from the patch-worked network of drainage rhines that covered the Somerset Levels. On a beautiful sun-drenched morning they shone like ribbons of light across the Moorland. Henry preferred Plot 43 but that had been rented to Old Bill twenty years ago and although Old Bill was twenty years older he hadn't changed at all. He was the same. His body hadn't changed. he still dug his spuds and grew his runner-beans from the same seed as his own father had handed down on to him.

Henry needed a new shed. One with a new felt roof tacked down with new, galvanised felt nails. All in shiny straight lines just like the rich guy's shed on Plot 4. There was a snag, no money. what little he had was spent on rent arrears and excuses for late payments for other things like the washing machine that was a dire necessity when his beloved wife, Nancy had passed away the previous year after catching something with a long word that the doctor had tried to explain.

Mandy worked hard all her life as a closer in the local Shoe factory. She had stitched her way on a flat-bed Phaff machine through countless miles of leather. Calf skin, snake skin, cow-hides from South America and even for the super-posh styles, the skins of baby lizards. Her back had taken the very stance of leaning forwards for so many years that she was now a bent and buckled woman. No longer was she the 'Factory Pin-up Belle', she walked with the low-down stoop of a lonely low-down tramp almost thinking that begging would benefit her income but she was too proud to do that. She had dreamed of a brand new carpet for her sitting room. One with a bright floral blaze of red roses woven within the fabric. One just like her mother had in the old family home when she was a little girl, and just like that little girl that still lived deep in her memory on quiet Sunday Mornings, when there was no-one around to see, she could get down on all-fours and count each blaze of colour by pointing them all out with her index fingers. Money was needed and with the expensive underlay and fitting costs it looked like the only flowers she'd be seen counting were the ones that grew in the hedgerows.

She was unable to sew anymore. The Arthritis had made sure of that but she kept her old Singer machine on a table at home like any other great achiever keeps a sporting trophy. It didn't gather dust. Trophies never gather dust and deep within our hearts we can relive the moments on the presentation day when we all had a place to look down on others. Mandy wanted her dream to come true so the extra money was at least a start...

Margo had a name to befit her career. She had been a model and dress-designer in her working life. Fifty years ago, or was it Forty? She had walked around the edge of the Lido displaying a shocking two-piece bikini! Everybody talked about that day. The day when if your midriff was good - the one piece costume died.

She had become somewhat an expert at helping the larger-lady with an outfit that flattered an obese figure. Larger ladies that didn't go to fashion shops for fear of being stared at by the slimmer, younger girls who would giggle as they ate the fat-soaked burgers that would eventually judge them also.

Margo had her dream. A visit to London but not to purchase anything. She just wanted to visit the big fashion houses and look at all the amazing garments hanging still-less on plastic stone-faced manikins. To look and imagine herself walking the cat-walks bathed in subtle spotlights and hear the gasp of the audience as she stepped out from behind the screens.

A journey like that would involve a great cost. The bus to the station, the long train journey and the booking of a cheap hotel, somewhere near the shops and if she's enough cash, a trip to the theatre to see "The Mousetrap". To the theatre to remember when Dicky took her arm in arm and he was so dashing then in his white dinner jacket, slicked back hair and straight waxen moustache. She'll remember his charm and the familiar smell of theatres as all good theatre-smellers do. Just like those good old days she could highlight her cheekbones with a touch of rouge to enhance her fading beauty.

Today though she kept her dream safely written down and folded with other papers and Kodak photographs in a beautiful Edwardian writing slope that Dicky had given as a special present on the day before the train crash. The day when he failed to meet for tea and cake. The day when a great piece of her lifestyle was lost forever.

Today she was making a positive start to ensuring that all these wonderful things would happen.

Henry, Mandy and Margo didn't really know one another. It was not important. It might interfere with their dream spaces. Today they all worked very hard in the local supermarket stacking shelves way into the night. The money was going to come in handy....

News from Hell 2016

He's delivering the News again,
I am so Hungry in bed —
I wish he'd deliver a Pizza instead.
A council letter from Mendip.
Alas no savoury dip.

No Marmite journey on my bread
They're now shooting from the hip,
"Can you sign here" he said

Abandon Ship!

News 2016

I heard you say,
Just the other day,
That something had died,
Under this sky I wondered,
As the heavens thundered
And thought of it and cried.
Everything changes and goes too soon,
Like resting feet in the Afternoon
When there is so much to do.
How can it help us now?
It has died — as all things do.....

I'll remember its face,
Staring back at me.
It's lines and proportions,
Of symmetry.
The times when I summed it all up.....,
Mystery.
Didn't fathom out its thinking,
I was too busy, drinking.

Today you rang to tell,
It had heard the calling Bell
Had gone to catch the last train,
Didn't even leave a parting note,
Of when it'd be home again
But there are times when all things leave
Makes us sit up and Wonder...,
Makes us grieve.
Makes us sit and knowingly sigh

That although its gone
Something also deep within us die.
"God rest ye Merry Gentlemen
Goodbye my favourite Pet Goodbye,"
Amen.

On Shelley   2016

I recited "The Cloud" to her.
She'd got a First in English
        in those Winchester days.
She was marrying another,
Waking up with me
Didn't seem to bother.
They'd fed her those words
And she'd learnt to detest him. —,
But, - "THE CLOUD" was new
        To her streets
As we shared the same Bed sheets
A bit of Shelley,
And evening with George Melly,
The students said he was an old man,
Like falling of a log,
They didn't understand.

Service   2016

I suppose a cup for two pounds Sterling,
Isn't worth your wait,
To switch on and Make
  My morning.

A family of four
With tea and cakes and ices —,
Is worthy of the Attention Deficit
A whole table where they sit
In other peoples' clothes
  the Staff here know —,

Just jumping to attention!
  "The coffee, Waitress please?"
  or did I fail to mention.....?

Silk   2016

Silk is the best thing to wear —,
It slides over your Nakedness.
With a coiling gentle grip —,
Gives life Body —.
Gives life Form —.
Opulates Venus —,
The girl you live with.
Disregard
       The Laundry ticket
Cardboard and Dry
Edge-sharp as her words
When she read the price-tag....
Her garments are from "The Good House"
Somewhere in London
British Home Stores?
       I do not think so —,
I sit there!
In Silk sliding my Way
Snakelike to the girl working the till:
"One coffee in a straight glass oh!
       with tap water"
I don't pay mineral prices.....
       Venus wears Cashmere
Sits upright even when she's cleaning.
       Venus wears Roses
I don't like things that die.
       Venus wears Dead Roses.
"Don't they smell nice?"
"Like a grave." I said,
       Lie them to Rest

In the Cemetery with the Others
      I found earlier.
Dead flowers and Silk
A calamity in the dark
Where the shadows
Of the dying Larch
Claw fingers on the street-lit path.
The Owl cried out:
"Silk is the in-thing!
Wear always next to Noses
And not dead flowers —
LIKE ROSES!"
"What does **He** know?" Venus said.
I thought he was better than her.
At least he could fly.......

St. John's Church Glastonbury 2016

A great Stone.
Peoples' graves.
Winding Maze.
Lost wordings on Headstones
People lying on People-bones
Children's voices by the Daisies
Corner tree full of Crazies.
St. George's Chapel Schh! —,
NO TALKING OR PRAYING ALOUD.
Write a message for a loved one
Drive away the haunting Drum.

St. Michael's looking down on You
Weighing you up — he's no fool.
He looks upon me as I stand
Doesn't scare me! —,

You cannot weigh the soul of a just man.
Two old Biddies in the corners
"Four o'clock!" they call last orders.

Talc or Oil Sir?   2016

I desperately need a Woman!
To take this Pain away
She was caring —,
I laid on the couch staring
          At a Mobile
She said that kissing doesn't hurt
As she pushed the Needle in.
What sort of date is this? —,
(She looked good in the Photograph)

I got my fetish for uniforms as a boy in the Army
          and she,
The girl with the Manacles arrested
My desires with Morphine
as she stared at my face.
She's got a nice complexion, no spots
          I could judge
As she examined My scarring that
I'd had a troubled Adolescence
"This won't hurt one bit"
The liar......
          Girls are all the same
She took a souvenir of our meeting
A momento
For her Trophy Collection
"Only a tooth" she said.
"Not bad..." I thought —,
The last girl took my heart....

The Church Visit   2016

She told me.
She sold me
But I wasn't for Sale.
Got my own Belief
I say it with Relief
By this mug of Ale.
THAT WOMAN relayed Church News
Told me they'll remove these Pews.
Need a concert somewhere to perform
What was wrong out on that lawn!
Blame the Victorians, they put them there!"
        she said
I looked blankly at her blaming
        someone else instead.

A devout Christian with a mission
As feral to life as the Jew that goes hungry.
She said that many times she'd seen
        me before
I said "Yes, I am familiar with that door
Even when it's locked —,
Like a gun that's cocked —,
Ready to fire unexpectedly in your face.

"Always take careful aim when choosing
your religion
Lest, we all go without."

I told her that I had bills to pay.
She said the weather's lovely now —,

An Indian Summer full of Cowboys
Still patching up life
With the Wrong Glue.

I told her my Mother was dying.
She said she'd crocheted a coat
Winter can be colder here Sometimes.
I told her my best friend was troubled.
She said she often did the Daily Crossword
She found that helps.

"Always take careful aim when choosing
your religion
lest, we may never see heaven."

She asked me if I'd like a tea
She was fresh out of Prayers.
But maybe,
Maybe a Sandwich instead.
"I made them earlier in the Vestry."
What's the flavour?
"Mandrake," she said.

I told her I was Corrupted.
She said there's a lot of that going about.
Didn't think it's catching though.
Look, I've made a Credit Card
With this old church Jukebox.
The slot no longer accepts money
Definitely not foreign stuff
That's used to purchase Communion Wines
That Shopman never notices
Maybe he's afraid of God sometimes.

"Always take careful aim when choosing
your religion
Lest, you'll be blamed on a technicality."

I told her I was the Son of God.
She remarked on the Likeness.
Said I looked like a picture in the newspapers.
That he was popular too
He was wanted.
       The Pews will be going
To line a brewery floor with beer.
Maybe refit the Brothel
Where the Merchants' go.
When they're not selling things here.
Maybe make Clogs so the Poor are Shod.
I came into this Madhouse knowing.
I'll sit at the Right-Hand of God.

"Always take careful aim when choosing
your religion
Lest, we all start to notice things
and feel a sense of Shame."

I told her of the latest Massacres
In Syria or some other place I've never heard of.
She said her washing's dry
It's such a lovely day!

"Always take careful Aim when choosing
your religion
Lest, you'll be blamed for being a Christian."

The Language of Birds   2016

In the Olden Days
There were No trees
So the birds just had to Walk
The ground was sharp and prickly
So then they learnt to Squawk.

> A chicken ran by with a Mutter
> "Poor diction" said the Owl
> "Please try your best to Clutter"
> "And as for all you others,
> Talk properly too"
> It then sat up straight and said:
> Twit - ter- woo

The Great Auk's Squawk
The Robin's trills
The Hoards of Crying Seagulls
Far over the Hills —,
>   And not forgetting Jenny Wren
HERE SHE IS! Oh...,
>   She's gone again.

The Lights go out - Even in Folklore   2016

After the Rain
The Earth Wall Collapsed
A dull and solemn thud against her door.
        Celeste she's standing
        by the window
I try not to notice her
She always stares at me
Some distant memory
When I was light years away
And she was from Another Planet.
I regret that day
that evening when my words tripped on hers
        As she Sang in the Back Bar
So much so
        that she never did forgive me.
Writhing Blonde Medusa-headed girl
Scared the shit out of me!
I tried to Ring a mate in Athens for help —
But he'd died a Thousand Years ago.

The Vented rage that spurs her Anger
At my refusal at the first Hurdle
When my Soul pulled back short
Of another grip 'tween those constricting legs.
That Steed may have stumbled and fell
As he gave me an Apology
But I walked away from that Race
Unharmed
The Vet turned up and without much fuss,
Put it down.

I'd heard of a Man who was Strong
"Thank God" I said moving Decay
      from A to B
I needed a hand with the Fridge
Although busy helping the Farmer
With a crazy clearout he came
      Mumbled....,
      Grumbled....,
Made complaints about the Druids
Told me the lions needed feeding
Moaned on..... and... on.... and On!
About his love for Another.
I didn't understand the Guy
It was all Greek to me.

It'd be nice

It'd be nice if it were sunny everyday
And it'd be nice if my love loves me for always
And it'd be nice to be forgiving to the ones that I love most
It'd be nice to be winning all the time

It'd be nice to be wealthy all my life
And it'd be nice if people stop giving me grief and strife
Oh but sometimes, oh sometimes I just can't get it right
It'd be nice to be right all the time

The Odd Couple   2016

I know I am much Older than You
        But,
You can wrap me in a blanket —,
Or whatever's at Hand.
Put me in the Beach-house —,
You can play on the Sand.

Wear your favourite Kaftan
Or whatever's at Hand.
You can rub my bones Younger
Teach me again to Stand.
We'll danse the way Français
To Trenet's "Le Mer"
Others watch us questioning —,
They can stare.
At your Beauty that gives me Zest!
The beating of the Brass-band.
You're the one I live for —,
Or whatever's at Hand.

The Opening Ceremony   2016

Readers' Note: A Royal Visit to open some form of Iron and Steel Industry up North. Painfully executed by a member of some Royal Household through a sheer lack of Boredom. Such is the futile interest of the Monarchy deep within a wasteland that once provided the community with work.

The Opening Ceremony

Who are we to Judge you now?
The wheels of industry red rusting labours
Of lost eternities
Quicklime the Blisters burn better with
Fork-tongued Uncertainties.
The Magistrate choked on Gabel
Crumbling loose Foundation Stone
Stumbled on his regalia maybe he'd
        grow into them
Meagre dinner-plated workmen
Stumbled in the Heat
Life is forgiving the Dustmen's throat
Set ablaze the parting iron shield
Upon the very faceplate looking —,
Staring at you my friend,
        then Another.
Who's heart can Yield the Fledgling
        sparrow Gable the pipe
That sent the river back to beach
To lonely outcrops this stillness
Never hurt no man nor Beast.
Ivory smooth the lintels released
    a Breathe
The Cannon Foundry short of war

       fired loud
Dust Cloud steeped
       with Cheap Woman's perfume
And the Air was Released.
Harken well you crowd-lined pockets
Flag-waving her visit when she came.
That Black Car held her body still
As if a Funeral Hearse had been ordered
Little signs of life bar
A parting wave.

The Price of Air   2016

How much do we really need?
How much do we want?
They Christened a baby today
Made a fuss beside the Font.
Cradled the little bugger
        When it cried,
Lit a candle for its life — I know that Vicar
He often lied.
All around him Knew
He didn't fair too well at Sunday School.
And Debbie chastised the prophets
For getting drunk again
"Let's hear it for the BOYS! ~ " "Amen."
They'll light another
When he turns Old
Wheel him up to that Altar,
Memories, stories told,
Wheel him in on the Great Gun Carriage,
Say little of his loveless marriage
Absent son and Daughter
How much money do they really need?
When there are countless mouths to feed
Heavens Above!
One guy promised Eternal Love.

The Wound 2016

The Wound did not Heal
It festered in the Summer
Coming out in Wintertime to Cry
Called against the Ironed will
Breached across the untamed Skin
Created a Rash
Upon the Body
      When the septicaemia crept In.

The Pretty nurse of Foreign Caste
Drew back the Curtain
The others looked on, uncertain....
      if I'd made it through.

The Vicar shouted Revelations
About our Faith in Fairy-tales
Of turps and paint and all things clinical,
Dr. Thompson turned up too
Bollocked the churchman for being cynical,
Told the Nurse to shut the Windows
You never know which way the Wind blows?

The Wound did not really Heal
The Captain said it would
Muttered something about healing
As if he knew he could
Told me of life's long plan
Staged his latest Strategy
Within this Foreign Land.

The Wound did not go
It hides within the leather
Fashioned Officers' Mess
Inside the very fabric
Of the latest plans and attacks
There's Shepherds grazing with their sheep
They're hiding in the cracks
Making bread with a dull flour
Chewing Mouths full of dead flowers
Stolen from their unmarked Graves.
Calling out to the Open Sky
Like us; they too,
Know Jesus Saves.

The Poet   2015

Your presence was dull
and —,
Your recital also.
Like an excited crow
That's found a dead rabbit
You jabbered and hopped to perform
In front of a murdered audience.
Your style was so predictable —
It became stiff and lifeless.
You body gave away the smell,
That you were dead and all your friends
Performed your animations....

To Whom We Serve 2016

She follows me as this minioned River chained
to servile aging banks.
About to fall away,
The decay, of Willow-roots
Harbour onto an unsafe anchorage
Of undiscovered Faith in what I am doing,
Of what I am up to as if —,
I could hold back the rising Floodwater.

What is this smell, this strange scent
That gases Us? —
What is this flavoured inspiration?
That binds us as I,
Even in separation,
Find such a difficulty to mention at the table?

You said your belief in Saints was sound
When you played the Crucifixation,
On our Wedding Day. Kneeing —,
For a blessing
As if we believed
It could repair the imperfections.
Silent as the Dove's whisper
When it was trampled down by this River,
On this Day of surprises
When even the moon
Has turned to Glass.

Waiting for War   2016

The Old boys had their scars the
New recruits had nothing better than Acne and a heavy rifle.
          "Fasten Your Clips," the Sergeant said.
Young boys looked down —,
Their belts were fastened tight as
          Mother-hugs at leaving time.
The Salt Road beckoned
Beer still hangs in Young Men even at noon.

The Old boys, one will be thirty soon
Hard on words.
Hard on Young Boys.
Can penetrate thoughts as easily as Steel
Piercing the odd body or two
Coughed on Older lungs thinking —,
Maybe they should give them up —, Pass the packet.

Give us time.
Give, us time.....
There's people - Insurgents outside Sir —
          they're making a racket!....
Give it time Boy
Give it time for time will tire them down
Then we'll go to meet them.
Let's just sit here awhile
The Back-ups on Order - with deserts too I hear!

Give it time Boy
Give it time —,
No time to fear...

What's Up Now 2016

How much do we really need?
How much do we want?
I offered you Paradise
Look clearer through your Eyes.
Can't you seen that Woodland Clearing?
Remember your Childhood and all that Yearning
Smell my lawns beneath your Feet
Think of what we Share that —,
Makes Life so Sweet.
See a thousand sights in One
Look at all that has begun.
Hold me when your falling
I am always there —,
Stroking your soft greying hair.
Think of the Morning,
Dreams that gave you fright.
Then look, and look again at me —,
Everything comes Right.
The Whispers in ears.
When everyone around us was gaining
You know I'll get up soon
Unless it's raining.
I'll work when the mood takes me
Especially when the Cupboard's empty.
Buy you wine and bread.
Hold a candle to your kind of Worship
Maybe buy the dog a bone
If he's earned it.
What on Earth do people need
When they are Happy.

Vegetarian BBQ   2016

"Pass the Burgers! What's in them?
Hmmmm.... It's missing something??"
"Sauce,
Red or Brown?
We've Mayonnaise also —
They call it Mayo in this Town.

That's a bit Up-Market — the figure of Speech and all
"What does it taste like?" she said,
Hints of subtle Parkay Floor
Undertones of Elderflower
Full of under-currents
DON'T GO IN THE BURGHER - YOU'LL DROWN!
Call the Life-guard they cried
Reaching out for Saving Grace
And you know what her dad did? —,
Caught Fish.
Big fat-battered fryers, grill or oven bake
We use to buy Cod
But reluctantly eat Hake.

"That's an oily fish"....
Better than this dish
          there's nothing in it but,
Rabbit Food.
I am Shape-shifting!
Hop... Hop... Hop.......

Why on Earth do You do this?   2016

If it wasn't for Poetry I would have crept off and died on some
forbidden landscape with the words of Coleridge and Elliot buried in
my dead head.
It's hard to go it alone. I always treasured company. The girls I
shared bread with gave me more than an appetite. They swelled my
senses. Gave me a foundation to base my sanity on. I suppose I miss
them all but only one can I define as true love because I still miss
her. I think of her every day, it gives me a false sense of security of
belonging to something. She is gone but it's a bit like death — we
never really say 'goodbye' — more like, "see you later...."

The View from Here   2016

I have always had my visions. Others have dreams.
　　A dream is something that usually happens when eyes are
Closed, a bit like tugging on a Wishbone if you're lucky ——, and
it's your turn in the queue.
　　A vision is a true picture of what WILL happen. It's not a
perceived idea. It's something that's possible if acted upon. how
many times have dreams and visions faded away? ... Too Often.
　　I get a funny feeling deep within me that for a long, long time
——,
We have ignored the voice of God....
　　There is Nothing wrong with going hungry for anything. It's
on tomorrow's menu boards —,
　　"Didn't You see the Signs?"

The Tea Party   2016

George was meticulous in his work and spent countless hours a day deep underground in the dark often lonely bunker of an office. Age had bettered his ways and he often thought that the surge of New Technologies had by-passed him. His knowledge of computers was empty and as far as he contented, they just did not exist. Like anything else within the glossy magazine that slipped out of his Sunday Papers it all fell seemingly with a dull thud on his earth floor. Only to make his body cuss as he stooped down to pick them up. He also tried to find others things to pick up whilst he was visiting the foot department of his life.

George was from the old world where strict methodical and systematic planning and record keeping was all done on paper. Boxes in columns and ticks upon charts were carefully entered skilfully with a sharp HB pencil. This would allow for the odd correction to be done just as skilfully with an eraser. Little Jenny, as his subordinate, was prone to the odd error of judgement and because she was young and pretty, he always forgave her imperfections.

Technology may have advanced more than the mould creeping up the wall in the far corner next to the waste-bin. Technology with its latest plasma flat screen was no different to George's flat-screen. He referred to it as "The Wall". That hadn't changed. It was flat, well, apart from around the hole that was somewhat uneven. He didn't care for that blemish for he spent the off-times when he wasn't overworked by peering through his "interesting circle" as he had called it when it first appeared after a heavy downfall of rain. The whole world had gone bonkers with all the downloading onto files when, with a gentle push or pull, the filing cabinet with the squeaky sliders did just the same job! And, if it wasn't in that cabinet, it was in his long pointy head. Full of long, pointy brain materials.

Young Jenny came creeping into the office. She usually bounced into the space wriggling her hips in a fashion that displayed the flirtation of the young that go the distance to attract promotion within the workplace.

"Jenny dear, you look a little dry today. Go and lie down in the cupboard space for a while. It's quite refreshing and you'll soon be writhing around again in your normal self" he turned, rearranged his reading glasses which had tilted across his face as they often did when he looked upon young Jenny.

He did not know why? But put it down to the memories of his own youth. The days when he could wriggle also.

His desk was unique. George had designed it all by himself. It had a flat top and four stout legs all the same shape and size. He never referred to it as the desk, he called it "the table"... Everybody else had desks and he didn't want to be like them. Everybody else's tables were made of cold, boring metal. George knew better than them —. Metal rusted and had sharp nasty corners. Wood was the correct material and when it rotted away he could use it for other just as useful things like for making soft pillows for the little ones that lived in the nearby complex of housing. Yes. George's table was special. It was so special to him that he gave it a name - Eve, and George and Eve got on really well together and never argued as most couples did when they worked close to each other.

Jenny came into the room feeling much livelier. She curled her body around George and gently handed him something.

"More paperwork Jenny! Why didn't you put it in the 'IN' tray? You know my system of order?" George looked up at the ceiling, surely she didn't need further training? He was unsure if the meagre budget could fund another course of instruction.

"It's not paperwork Mr. George. It's a present for you for being so nice to a pretty little thing like me."

George opened the neatly wrapped package wondering to himself where she had got the wrapping paper from.

"It's a COMB! What am I going to use a comb for? You can see quite clearly that I am BALD!"

"I thought that you could keep things stored between its tiny compartments like people do" sighed Jenny.

"Like what?" enquired George.

"Head lice."

He opened an old cabinet marked with an old label titled "THINGS I DON'T WANT TO LOOK AT EVER AGAIN" and filed it away next to the ring tops and 'interesting but useless plastic things'.

Work had to be done. The light that usually streamed through the cracks in the ceiling was fading and even George knew that it always was very difficult to read in any other unlit rooms also - he didn't like carrots. The rabbits in the Park were well-read. They could read in the dark. They ate carrots! George didn't care much for rabbits. They didn't have a posh office like his. He never really cared about well-read rabbits. They may read a lot on farming and selective breeding but they couldn't write. Have you ever seen a rabbit writing a letter yourselves? I didn't think so.

Jenny looked up above her pen. Her beautiful dark eyes dilating at the power of Mr George's presence or did they just dilate due to the lack of light? She didn't know but was still transfixed on Mr George. He was so clever!

"Mr. George sir? Mr. George sir? Mr. ....."

"Yes Jenny. What is it THIS TIME!"

George flapped through loose paper. It had to be correctly filed away under SECTION 2B.

"Can we have an Office Party?"

"Jenny —, even you know what happened at the last office party. There was all the tidying up afterwards and nobody turned up to help —, and that young blonde ran off with that office boy and it completely ruined so many people's lives," sighed George as he wondered if it all had a happy ending.

"But Mr. George.... you promised us all that you'll surprise us one day?" said Jenny as she turned on her sad face that usually did the trick.

George thought his surprise was introducing longer working hours then thought again that in order to motivate his workforce that they needed at least some form of reward. He'd read about it in a book on the Psychology in the Workplace that had fallen through the roof onto him many years ago.

"Okay - I give in to your request. Tell all the others to meet in the Great Chamber tonight at six o'clock for an important meeting."

He looked around to hand her jacket that was hanging on the back of her chair - but she was gone.

George like promptness and punctuality. He was always standing waiting his turn to board a train or city bus but never quite managed the journey because of his height. That's the trouble with being an Earthworm, nobody really notices your face peering through the cast-iron drain plate. Nobody realises the trouble you took to even arrive, let alone depart. Tonight though all he had to do was lock up the Office and worm his way over to the Great Chamber, and easy distance and they would all be there waiting excitedly for his announcement.

The Great Chamber shone out a faint beacon of hope for an office party. The glow-worms had arrived extra early to provide the blessed light. They were careful and conscientious folk who often guided many a bewildered worm homewards on many a dark foreboding night. They cared also for the needy and often gave interesting flashing displays within the hedgerows to the fascination of the tiny little wormlings that peered through tiny little windows afraid of going outside in case the Black Shadows took them away. The Black Shadows were stealthy and silent and were the harbingers of doom. They were rarely talked about, but everyone knew they existed.

From out of a small crevice appeared a multitude. A swirling, spinning mass of Woodworms carrying small bark hampers for their own refreshment. An important meeting always was a sure indication that everything came out of the woodwork.

The woodworms had covered a long journey to attend and listen to the wisdom of George. they usually lived in the old potting shed at the bottom of the garden and had followed an old shadow path which led them at risk to the Great Chamber. Luckily for them they all had arrived safely. No lives were lost.

A festering smell of damp, musty air filled the Great Chamber as all eyes gathered to focus on the Great Top Table. A special place decked with sparkling cobwebs and glistening glow-worms that twinkled like lost stars within the heavens. Amongst the loose chatting of worm-woman's words could be heard a different sound. The creaking hulk of something that was the great possessor of words and reasons. The Office Manager. The Great Old Worm, George.

He stretched his segmented body straight to display his authority within his community. A community usually lost in the great vastness of Mother Earth. A community that mined the hardened soil to manufacture it into the stuff that gives all greenery life-giving wonder. A lifetime of turning and drilling deep into the sub-surface of the world to create sustenance for the benefit of Men and their animals. The unpaid employees to their God. The makers of the finest earth and humus - the most savoury and tasty vegetative mould that all plants longed for and dreamed of.

George looked up from the sticky paperwork that was stuck fast to his upturned tail, adjusted his glasses and, when the noise subdued and all that could be heard was the stillness of the night, that gentle hiss deep within the middle ear - spoke.

"Friends and baby wormlings! Thank you for coming to this somewhat impromptu meeting. Why, I must confess that if it hadn't been for young jenny's request this meeting may never have happened. You know how busy I usually am sifting through various work schedules and maintenance programmes. I had overlooked my biggest job requirement. To ensure the welfare of not only my employees but also to all that visit or reside here in this growing industrialised community. Tonight, when darkness falls and the grassy lawn is wet with evening dew we are going out to a party!"

The Great Chamber erupted into a spasm of spiralling excitement. Some worms even fell off their chairs in surprise. Baby Wormlings wriggled seed rattles in praise to the 'big old worm' (as they were known to call him).

"I've noticed many friends from afar have journeyed to be here. News certainly gets around the Grapevines here. The Brandlings are here in their beauty. Dressed in your vermillion robes with yellow ribbon bands wrapped around your bodies. The Great Lob-worms, my relations, are seated there at the back of the Chamber on the harder seating. The Woodworms have done their usual party trick - I notice a table's already missing!

Now for my other dearly loved friends and soul-mates - the Glow-worms which brings me to mention something that may shock you all.

The Glow-worm as we fondly call them, is really a beetle! Well I never! The man that decided to call a beetle a worm must surely need to see his optician! Never mind —, over the centuries everyone refers to you has lowly worms when really you should have the glassy-shelled splendour of something far more beautiful. Dear Glow-worms, dear, dear friends, if it's okay with you it would be my greatest honour to always refer to you as worms."

A burst of vivid light filled the room highlighting many a bald head. The Glow-worms turned up their tiny flashlights to maximum settings to display their approval at being accepted for just being what they are.

"Now", said George, "I want you all to form a line in a minute."

"Can we do it now Mr. George?" enquired an eager Jenny.

"No! —, listen!"

Above their heads could be heard a snuffling sound. The vibrations shook some earth loose and it fell heavily from the earthen roof.

"It's the Badger!" shouted the throng of writhing visitors.

"It's doing his usual patrol, and, on time too! You could set your sundials to his punctuality," said George as he lovingly patted the Wormlings heads to take away their fear.

"Give it a couple of minutes and it will soon move on to the Great Meadow that separates us from the Black Stone road."

The vibrations and sounds drifted away and everything became calm again.

"Now! You can form lines but follow me because I know the Straight Path which always proves to be the shortest route."

George rubbed a little fresh slime into his dry, cracking body then wormed his way to the Great Wormhole's entrance. A useful hole with many purposes. It allowed a thin trickle of rain into the Great Chamber to maintain a worm-ambient temperature and the free passage of cool air on hot, humid nights so as to promote better sleeping conditions and aid slumber.

Peering out George surveyed the landscape. The wheelbarrow had been moved but apart from that everything looked in order.

"Follow me," and he slid boldly out into the night.

The evening air was fresh and after being underground for so long, — refreshing. In the distance stood a large stone tower, and outside the large stone tower with its painted door, shone a bright light. This was the tower of man the possessor of fire and light!!! George had often a-spied him sitting in his tower by the window reading from well-bound leather books. A fortunate man who lived alone amid the paintings of a former life as an artist.

"Is he at home Mr. George?" enquired young Jenny as she skidded on the slug-trails playing sliding games with the little ones.

"No, Young Jenny. He's gone away to recite poetry at the 'Great Festival of Has-beens' in another country.

"But —, he's left the lights on" said the girl as she picked herself up after a foolish skid disaster.

"He's prone to do that. It's a habit of his. I think it's there to welcome him home on his return. I read somewhere that he once had a family but they vanished one day in something that divorced him of who he really was. That's why he always leaves the radio on... It makes him believe that they're still really there."

"Is he happy Mr. George?"

"Yes, I think so. He's learnt to laugh at himself aloud again."

An attack! A silent attack! In a split-second one of the crimson Brandlings disappeared. Then another.

"Take cover!" shouted George "It's the Dark Shadow Calling!!"

The Dark Shadow picked out many wormy souls before everybody found safe hiding places.

"Where does it come from?" whispered Young Jenny.

"Down from the Great Open Sky" said George peering up to the heavens cautiously waving his tail to give the signal that it was okay to move on.

The Stone Tower was so high that it melted away into the night but on the door was skilfully fitted a flap.

"He knows about us doesn't he Mr. George? He's even fitted a worm-flap to make his home more accessible when his door isn't open."

"He is very wise Young Jenny, I've even seen him looking after Peacock Butterflies during the cold winter months. He allows them to hibernate on his bathroom ceiling. It's cold there so they don't wake up until the warm Springtime comes again."

On entering the Tower all the crowd gathered in the corner of the kitchen. The smell was absolutely amazing! Old dusty bread, rancid butter and better still - rotten potatoes in a large wet brown bag on the floor!

"Welcome Worms to the Grand Annual Works Party! Feast yourselves on such a banquet of decaying waste!"

Everybody just piled in. A perfect dinner and music to wriggle their best moves to.

"Come with me, I've an even better treat. Can you smell that sweet vapour?"

"What is it?" asked a multitude of worms all at the same time.

"Earl Grey tea-leaves! Judging by the scent I would say that it's very old rotting Earl Grey. It's up there in a strange shaped pot in the window."

Slithering up an old water pipe they made the great assent to the overpowering aroma of something almost Continental. Past the fusty biscuit-barrow, the empty wine bottles with dregs of a dull pallor stained upon the glass. The bone-dry dishcloth draped limply over the cold tap. Dead flowers and old dusty Christmas cards. To the pot smelling of ambrosia!!

"Here's the smell-pot, how do we get in?" said a very puzzled Young Jenny.

"Just over here is a long tube fitted to the side of the smell-pot" said Mr. George.

"It's a handle!" said a bewildered Jenny.

"THIS SIDE!!" said George fearing that maybe if she did have any hair that it would most likely be blonde.

They all slid up to the tube falling through the china hole into a bath of delight. Feasting and squirming in the essence of what could only be described as passion!!

Later that evening a car pulled up in the yard outside. It was the Man of the tower! Unlocking the door he entered and after a long drive home thought that it would be a good idea to make a cup of his favourite brew - Earl Grey tea. He took the tea-pot from the window and took off the lid and peered in. The worms looked up. The worms peered back wondering what would happen?

A rush of cold water gushed around them like a huge whirlpool of a crazy mixture. A journey to the hedge outside and the man banished them out to the soft soil.

"That was very lucky, very lucky indeed" pondered Mr. George as he gathered everyone ready for their journey back to the Great Chamber deep in the garden.

"Why was it lucky Mr. George?" enquired Young Jenny.

"He could have used hot water...."

The Prospective Buyer   2016

That Estate Agent worked Hard —,
He stuck the Picture on his Wall.
We stuck Knives and Spades in —,
Before the Fall....
> They're Shouting in The Stock Exchange:
> "Euros and Pounds!
> Euros and Pounds!"

The GDP is like your Postman —,
Just doing the Rounds.

"If blood is Shed we know it'll go well."
The Spokesman there is Calling:
> "Bring Out Your Dead!
> Ring! ... Ring...!
> The Pound is Falling!!"

"Let Blood now be Shed."

That Estate Agent worked Hard —,
> he visited.
Used a Fancy Tape-measure —,
To us it made little Sense —,
We knew the Distance.

That Buyer's not Certain if he'd settle down Here.
He's researched Men and Local Beer —,
A Missionary by Trade.
We told Him "no-problem"
It's a well-used position here.

"Upstanding?" he frowned
"No —, we usually do it lying down.

"How Remarkable!
Why, — if you performed like that in Africa,
Nothing short of a Miracle!
            — "What Religion do you follow?"
The Path in front Our face....
"But that Gutter's dripping
On You Saints —!"

We use Saint proof non-drip Paints.

"We'll take a Good Percentage!
We'll take a Small Percentage!"

Cheap suited Guy, cheap Shirt
Never really done a day's Work.
"If Blood is Shed it'll all go Well"

            —, I wasn't in Xanadu all the Time,
Just getting Visions from the Shelf
With that Girl —,
I a Cheap Hotel.

Tea for Two   2016

Never leave me here Again
By myself at the Tea-Room.
Turning around to see the View
                    but —,
Really looking out for You.
To ask as if I didn't know —
            the usual question
"One lump —, or two?"

Never leave me this empty Seat
Here it is beside my feet.
The Waitress girl came
To ask my Order again.
I told her I was waiting for someone.
Here she comes! but no —,
It's that Pretty Waitress Girl,
For a moment I thought it was You
My Angel with the Golden Swirl.

Each day I come here with the paper
Ordering a crispy wafer
The one that makes my heart Stop
Sugared Cube fell in with Plop.
My Coat is a bit frayed
            does it Show?
You know better than me
You know how people think
Even had a good career
            non the less,
            Still Penniless, —

We always made it Here.
When life raced by in seconds,
I dared to ask that first dance.
The Evening Late Last Orders Calling
A lifetime's Romance.
I waited there outside Your house
As furtive as a homeless mouse
The Street light's pale flutter
Me, standing there beside the Gutter.

The Window is bare
Save for someone's argument
Outside he shouts "She's late!"
How did that Chap know I am waiting?
I do not even know him.
It must be my anxious Face
Is it Showing?

There's a table over there
            with a Reservation.
I think they may be expecting someone,
Just like our gathering - me and You
But you've missed the appointed time,
            — Half Past Two.

I've played with this sugar long enough,
Brown into White like stormy waves
On fishing-boats lost at Sea
Forever Jesus Saves.
Stirred the open boat of Sugar bowl
With Nickel-plated oar
Skulling on a still-less lake
With the Lady i adore.

"No real Silver-service here, dear"
We're the only Senior-silver service
        they attend to,
And, all those years ago we chose —,
        this very venue.
Why? —,
You said the Style was Continental.
How was I to know?
I've never been abroad.
Never thought I'd get on with Foreigners
But Mr Patel's Corner Shop he's different!
He seems to be doing well - that's Good!
I never believed they'd settle here - well,
In a White Neighbourhood.

Next to this place where we always sit,
I've left a space for Your Bag to fit.
Perhaps some thin toast would be okay,
That Margarine looks good today.
Two side-plates on a frilly border
A small pot of unknown size —
Well - you know me with These Eyes!
That's why you help with the Crosswords,
As if we ever had any.

It's your favourite picture.
Well —, you always said you liked it,
Just like my own opinion
On the Wallpaper
Never mind
I remember you wiping tears
We can learn to live with it
It won't need redoing for Years.

There's no telling —,
Especially with my Spelling.

I ran my hand over this tablecloth.
"Chantilly Lace", the Song we laugh to
For our Kitchen dance, your unmarked grace
As you turned the Volume Up! —,
With that happy face.
Never <u>mind</u> the neighbours! Alas,
we have to put up with them cutting grass
On Sunday Mornings early dawn,
The only time we see them
Grooving on the lawn.
            Apart from their barbeque
When relations come,
When relations go,
When relations argue.....

            Where are You?
Where is that breath of Fresh Air
That stuns my senses?
My varicose girl
With the Twin-set and pearl —ed
Necklace that I stupidly bought
As a symbol of undying love.
When something more important than Gold-
Is having greater treasure to Hold.
The Waitress Girl came Again
She's as regular as the Weather,
Sunshine
Then Rain.
She said —,

"I bet she's ran off with some Feller!"

I couldn't find the strength to tell her.

Spare Part   2016

It wasn't easy to live life this time as a human. The last time had been much easier, I was just a part in a machine. I remember that happy time as a cog meshed to all the others and so long as we were well-oiled and occasionally adjusted by means of a spanner or hard knock against our cast-iron casing, we didn't complain. We worked non-stop for hours, only resting for holidays and of course Sundays when we all prayed to our Great Maker - Hornby Model Railways. We all knew his name. It was stamped below the tender clearly in bold print. Today I am human and in serious need of some education.

Here they come again looking down on me as I am imprisoned most of the time here in a Moses' Cradle. My name's Jimmy! — where did Moses come from? Perhaps to confuse the relations, who also look down on me and prod my face with big fat fingers. Here she comes again. The ugly one they call my mother. The other face is ugly too! I have been born into an ugly family. I wish I was a cog again. At least I could be engaged in something and whizz around on the railings scaring the cat. I wish I was a cog...

St John's Church   2016

I am sorry I was late Today —,
A funeral service got in the Way.
On Monday's I am always late.
Barred from entry, Padlocked Gate.
Keep the Sinner out
Let them stand elsewhere and Shout.
Let the Children play in the Street.
Not in here with Graveyard seat.

The Air was not Pure
Not from cleaner on the Floor
Someone's scent had filled the Room.
That smell of old ladies' perfume
A blight upon my tired breath.
But not like him — it brought him Death.
When all and One had gathered In
This place finally put an End to Him.
There are uncertainties
The People linger look at infirmities.
Someone's on the phone - a text.
Look my friends look on - who's Next?

"Excuse me but the Tearoom's Open Now?
Take a Pew
Here's a Menu"

Preparing for the Race   2016

Bitter seeds on Dry Palate
Wretched at the Nastiness the Commoner
Steeped herbs —,
        with tender loveliness.
A whiter shade of Green
Compared to Clinging ivy seen
On the Panelled fence.

"There are No weeds in God's Garden"

Bind-Weed high up in Rose
Trumpet-white the flowers sang
For Garden Hose.
All plants grow thirsty in this Heat Flowers die —,
        Even Roses.

"There are No weeds in God's Garden"

Bitter are the Apple Seeds
Plum too Almond fresh ingest bodies
        with poison. Arsenic.
Did the Wife we love know
        the distance run
Between Plum Pudding —,
        and Plain Dead?
Unaware as the suffering
Took over from the Racing on T.V.

As Saturday Afternoon
With Fag and Mag - the Racing's On!

It's 3 o'clock
It's G<small>RANDSTAND</small>!   and,
I am Galloping at
        New Market, Epsom and Chepstow.
Have you seen my form against your body —
As I move up in the Stall?
The Sweet Taste of Horse's Snot
Upon my Face
Can you smell it!
Can you smell my Success as I was
                Furlong Running.
I could have told you there
I cracked Whip on Bone
You didn't see me Coming!....

"There are No weeds in God's Garden"

I came aside just to catch your eye,
Was it squint or Wink?
Half-way in this Battle —,
Can't you hear my Death Rattle?....

She picked Mushrooms from under tree
The Birch-Wood didn't know
They never asked her anyway,
not even when it snowed...
"He likes his Mushrooms
Often meet with a friend to say
What's your Favourite Poison?"

Hedgerow Fodder - it's in Delia's
        or was Rick Stein's Book?
It's a well-used Mother's Recipe —,

I don't need to look..

"There are No weeds in God's Garden"

Lightly fry until half-cooked
It seals the Toxin in
Running the Distance - they're Necking
Fresh Runner-beans work well half-cooked
        When in Season —,
A dash of Lectin
           never hurt no-one.

That Mushroom worked
It's Hallucination Look! —
He's Riding 'BAREBACK' — on the Sofa
He loves his Horses
Loves early dinners too
Usually on a Saturday — three Courses will do...

"There are No weeds in God's Garden"

He's riding trim upon the Flat,
A Steeple-Chase would hurt his Back.
He doesn't do that anymore
Since the Accident on the Floor.

"There are No weeds in God's Garden"

On Missing   2016

You are Gone I miss You
Where is that quiet breathing
Against my Neck?
This Dark Winter longs for your Smile
Night,
Is Dark Night
Where is Your Light
That wakes me up to life?
But you are not Dead —
You have Not died —,
I heard you made him breakfast,
Fried.

On Age   2016

Old was Young the distances are few —,
They have their Wisdom —,
And days too.
       Written are the thoughts of Man.
Shifting,
Sifting
On this Wind-burnt Sand
        When no skin was giving
Save for a Path called Living.

There were No Songbirds in dark skies,
The Sea is Mourning
       a baby Cries.
Her beauty was so sweet —,
       I remember her.
Her Head in my Heart —,
       her Greying hair.
But now she is Gone
Somewhere where Doves Mourn —,
Coo.... is she?
Coo.... is she?
That diamond bright
That Majesty —,
       It sets my life alight
       Think of all those suitors
       You Put their feet to flight.

Old was Young their reviled Agonies
Leaned on Each other,
None were spared the Spear-edged Weapon
of Age its very beauty
Diminishing as the teeth in that
Beauty Pageant....,
                    — she too has died.
Her Fan-Club cease to Visit only the
Daily Helper with a fresh tin of spam.
Not too hard on gums —,
                    how's the Dentures?
Feeling much better,
They like to bathe in the Moonlight
I've heard from their Glass
                    they Stargaze
With a Broadway Smile.

All News is Good   2016

Nothing far Sweeter that life
Is your Smile
No matter what the Postman Brings —
you Smile...
Not everything is a present though
Look it's important!
It's got a Stamp
I know what's in them,
Known it all the While
And you gaze on adoringly and just —
Smile.

Oh Joy!   2016

Take me on The Swings Mr Rusty,
Take me to the Park,
You told me Of the Strangers there,
But Only after Dark.

Let me wash in Sunshine,
Let me Bathe in Rain,
I'll say sorry about the Carpets,
Won't do that Again.

Let me take Out all our Bread,
To throw up to the Sky,
There's so many Hungry Birds up there,
Look! - they're flying by.

Let me paint a Picture,
Colouring instead,
That drawing that I've told You,
Entering my Head.

Read me a Story Mr Rusty,
About the Times of Olde,
But never ever tell me,
That I am Growing Old.

Midget Gem   2016

There's a Midget living in the Hall,
Yes it's a Midget - very Small,
He's made a home in the Recycling Bin,
Disguised as a Bottle painted Green
It'll be quite hard finding him
He's the Same as all the rest
Making it hard from him to be seen,
Let's leave him be that'll be Best,
But Please don't discard him —,
                    Like the Rest.

In the Pet Shop   2016

Yes —, Birds I've had.
Two Cataracts.
Kept them for Years in a Bone Cage,
Should have been Gilded
Couldn't Afford to look after them.
Anyway —,
          They didn't do much over the Years
Just went more Opaque —,
Like a Cloudy Day.....

Le Café   2016

This is the Cafe I frequent
A place to sit and Germinate
Food, Warmth and Shelter
Eat the Food upon the Plate
Look up from my Paper
Notice the odd girl — her Mother!
Who makes me Wish
I wasn't old enough - to be her Father.

That Fan Above
Is the Only one I've Got
A small-Ad in the local
Might Secure a Slot.
I could being her Here!, —,
          Impress her,
Tell her about my love for Hemp Milk
With the expansive knowledge
Only Found on Stamps

I always take my Coffee Black,
Then it tastes like - coffee.

Killing Chickens   2016

That Old Bird I kept.
I loved her on a Whim
Soft-papered crumpled Mourning Sky
Brass yellowed Sunbeam stiff
As a man's arm with jaundice dead
Heaved life into the Harvest Shed
A farmer never gave up fight or flight.
The flightless birds stood no chance.
Wringing necks for Xmas tables
Within the Out-house Confined to Watcher's on
The Knife was sharp it bled lost tears Red
Upon Earth-floor rain pattered from the Dying-Feathered-Clouds
overhead
                    Brown hooks
Fastened taloned feet and Twine
To tie tight to the metal prison —,
Metal, as all Good Farming Men
When they're Killing Hen.

Women Folk came from the Village —,
There's talk today they're Clucking
Grab handfuls, tear down Straight.
A Morning Plucking and Blowtorch burn
What's stubborn to fingering.
Pluck them Whilst the bodies warm —,
Much easier than Prayer
When Reverend Tod had plucked up courage
I seen him through Corner eye
Standing there.

I Forgot to Say...   2016

She died in Sad October the leaves parting,
As the Door Opened.
Still silent air — at no cost,
Breathe upon Me in this quiet Hour.
        Dying always was —,
An extreme Way to say Goodbye....

"Who is it?" I say by the Haunted Gate
Patina smooth from your Unsteady Hand
Old iron squeaked —, cried "Out!" —,
As you Passed Wrought by Artisan's —,
Now Gone also as their Craft.

Clothes-brimmed Case —,
Carried Off your shroud.
White ribbons fluttered
On boughs where Prayers were Uttered,
Was this Day worth this Wait —
When Waiting Stiffens my Thoughts?
For Death —,
Takes you on the Boundary —,
And no time to say Goodbye....

We Played the Game
I caught you Eye
You caught my heart in Cricket
I had carefully Marked my Crease,
But You still took my Wicket.
My —, My!
        I saw you Die

As you triumphed on the Winnings,
And as I re-call —,
A fantastic score
The Umpire Agreed - a Good Innings.

     I had an Argument for You,
Rehearsed within my Mind,
You said:
     "When Your Quiets a Spoken Word —,
Bury Mankind"...

How to Write a Poem   2016

You know when you're little and have been to the Beach for the
Annual Family Day out — and you're excited! — You come back
home full of life!
You are Reborn!
You realise that Marvels are all around us!!
     You Bring that experience back. It lives in us for Days!! We
want to tell all our friends about this Wonderful Place.

     You bring home the Beach - In your Socks and Sandals. You
feel the salt-grit between your toes!
     You have lived! —,
     — Now You can Write.

His Comeback   2016

He turned up Again to spoil the Night.
Pre-booked —
       Still turned Up late.
Got through Holes in the Security,
Couldn't get my head around his Songs
Sung by the Old Man
               — who didn't care.
The Stage is Lit —
Where's the Spot to shine here?
On me, a STAR
         and you paying Fools Adorn
My Bank with Roses and Blue-notes
From the Cafe.
"Je suis un etoile!" — but...,
Never mind my bad language.

He's playing a Memory game
An old hit rendition
Of Pork, Of Wine with Undertones
And undercurrents
Of a Song he's drowning in.

Life has been good to him —, he's Fat.
Sits on his Cheeks
To hide his Face
And make a Mockery of Age.
There's the Shadow of a Star
Pretending on Stage......

Clió Loxton

Clió Loxton, born 28th May 1994, started life on her own at 16 years of age in Minehead, Somerset. The singer/songwriter has spent the years expressing her artistic side through music, art and writing poetry. The mother of two and much loved by her partner, she now resides in rural Devon working full-time as a restaurant manager and modelling in her spare time. Her friends describe her as on outgoing, funny and caring "breath of fresh air". She is also part-owner of a very proud father.

An Ode To The Black Death

Ye mayor has now caught the plague,
People shall flee far from town,
Everyone is ill and weak,
Now the mayor is struck down.

Parents hide from their children,
Anne Bawd her run from her mother.
This disease is swift and merciless
And unlike any other.

Slaughtering now in ye 1340's,
Some say 'tis a witches curse.
Others say 'twas anger of God
Which forces the world to yearn the dead nurse.

'Tis also said to run on rats but
The black plague, it moves by fleas.
It travels 'cross the country fast
Ye ones who know knock at the knees.

When you catch it, you get lumps.
Then thou shall cough up blood
And when thou die, thou shall join
Ye bodies lying in the mud.

If, however, thou should live,
Thou shall become immune to it
So that if it should come again
Thou shan't be in a body pit.

Folding Toilet Roll

Why do you fold your toilet roll?

Well...
Why do you make your bed?
Why do you plump the cushions on your chairs?
Why do you dust your shelves?
They do the same job if you don't.

Maybe I just like to know that
When the floor is covered in scrambled egg,
The highchair is plastered in ketchup,
The walls are spotted with...I don't even know what that is.

When toys are everywhere
And the bin smells of last night's particularly potent nappy,
Between the chaos of quarreling children
And after stepping on a thousand pens and dismantled clothes pegs,

When I do eventually manage to take two minutes to answer the call
of nature
At least I will be wiping my bum with flowers!

I Know Better

The thought of you
Is the fog on my mirror in the morning
It appears
Just as I think I can see what I'm doing
And without you
My mind is a blizzard of emotions blown up like dust in the sky
And when you're lying there with those puppy-dog eyes
I just want to be in your arms

And now I don't know whether I'm coming or going

I know I can't do this anymore
And I know you're the one I want most
But the only one I won't let myself have

Because I know better
I know better now
I know better
I know better now

I tell myself it's alright
I'll find someone new, so much better than you
One day
And I won't want to cry every time someone calls your name
But for now, in the present time
How can you expect me to be fine?
When you're lying there with those puppy-dog eyes
And I just want to be in your arms

And now I don't know whether I'm coming or going

And I know I can't do this anymore
And I know you're the one I want most
But the only one I can't let myself have

Because I know better
I know better now
I know better
How I hate that I know better now

And I want you but I know you'll only mess me around
And I'm fed up.
I'm fed up of playing swings and roundabouts
And I want you but no, now I can't let myself down
It's time to grow up now, I've got my own life I should be thinking
about

I should be thinking about how I know better

Loving you

You would like to see me cry
Over you
And you like to see me smile
At your command
And you love to see me dance for you
Sing for you
But you wouldn't like me to see
The things you do.

Well you sing your song of sixpence
With your pocket full of lies
And you pull one out your sleeve
And you cover up my eyes and you
Kiss me, so I can't breathe
So I'd never smell her scent upon your neck

You treat me like an infant
Like I'd never know the truth
And you spin your web of wonder
So I'd never see the blue
And your touch, so reassuring
Makes it better but these recurring
Instances are just deterring
Me from loving you.

Patch it up

If I could change your mind
By telling you a hundred thousand times I love you
I would

If I could change the ways of time
And undo all the bad things we've been through
You know I would

But it's shredded now
And you don't think there's any way to fix it
It's ripped at the seams
But you don't know what this means to me
How much I'll miss it

Let me take our torn design and make it something beautiful
Bright summer florals and winter blues
They all resemble me and you
And when we're together we can make a masterpiece
So darling, please, let me patch it up

Yes there's hope, don't give up yet
I promise that I'll not forget you're hurting too
But if you give me just one chance
I'll show you what we're missing
What we could do

And I know it's shredded now
And you don't think there's any way to fix it
It's ripped at the seams
But you don't know what this means to me

How much I'll miss it

Let me take our torn design and make it something beautiful
Bright summer florals and winter blues
They all depend on me and you
And when we're together we can make a masterpiece
So darling, please, let me patch it up

Peace – age 11

Peace
The swans on the still lake
The harmony of the two together
And so they shall remain
Their hearts entwined forever
The joining of two souls as one

Peace
The tranquil stream trickling down the hillside
The white fluffy clouds in the morning sky
The dawn chorus in the early hours of a new day
The crisp motionless air at daybreak
The night's dew on the grass

Peace
The silence at dusk
The birds singing in the trees in the evening
Shoals of fish elegantly shimmering in the sun
Never to be still
Always together as they twist around in the sea

Peace
A benefit of so many, yet lost by even more,
The beginning of war
Countless lives lost but now they shall rest in peace
Their souls now free from all grief and fear
A happier new life

Peace
The clearance of dust and rubble
The end of any question between life and death
Families rejoice and celebrate the magnificent day
The end of war
The wish of so many

Peace – age 21

What is peace?

Ten years ago it was the wonder of nature doing its thing, swans on a lake, fish in the sea and other standard topics. I wrote of the end of war, stuff like that. Cliché as it was, I was at peace just writing it. I remember. I had escaped and wandered around in my imagination for a minute. I knew it wasn't my greatest work but it made me happy. As far as homework went, I didn't resent it as much as I could have. I finished it and, quietly confident, I showed my mum.

I can still feel the sick embarrassment and gut-wrenching failure receiving her disappointment with me when she read it. Not the first time. That was her way. Sad really that homework meant so much; or was it my underachievement? I hated school. Maybe I'm starting to understand why.

I used to sing. I'd win competitions and do charity events. I'd sing in the stables, I was at peace there. The people loved it. Unfortunately after doing my second pantomime at fourteen, I vowed I would never sing in front of my mum ever again. Its one thing to want your child to do the best they can but coming to me as soon as I got off stage after my performance and reducing me to tears in front of the entire cast was too far by anyone's standards. I still don't understand why she did that. I was obviously upset at the fact I'd chosen not to do the splits during my act. It didn't matter that I pulled that muscle pushing my limits representing the county in athletics the week before. She had been pleased with me that week.

I will remember to praise my children for their efforts, not just their successes.

In hindsight, it's not hard to see why I couldn't write a peace poem.

I was subconsciously very confused and angry. I didn't know a thing about peace then. I just listed a series of romantic thoughts that I'd fabricated in my head. I don't think I really believed in any of it. I didn't know in my heart what peace was.

Now I do.

Now it's a bottle of wine and a hot bath alone when it's quiet at night.

It's the knowledge my partner has got the children while I fall asleep in the sun.

Peace is that sigh of relief when somebody else has done the washing up and, after a long and tiring week, getting to crawl into bed with my man on the precious nights when he's home.

Peace is not some great venture, some massive ideology that we should all try to achieve,

Its right here.

All you have to do is acknowledge it.

Pretty Little Thing

Like some wild animal; once bold, now shy
I hide away, lick my wounds and cry
And howl at the moon and talk to the stars
For what more company do I need than
A moth and a chance?

Still etched into my memory lies the haunting pain that you left me
It draws me in
To this fluttering fantasy where the nightlights all dance with me
And moth gives me a chance to see
What beauty can be

Pretty little thing
What could you take from me?
Spread your wings, we'll fly through the night
When I close my eyes from this last glance
Come on pretty little thing
What harm could you cause me?
If only in our dreams are we free,
Dream with me moth and chance

Ending just another tiresome day
As the sun's radiance fades away
I return to my dark, lonely home
And I can only wait until my body shakes with aches
And I'm tired enough to escape
To dream with moth and chance

Pretty little thing
What could you take from me?

Spread your wings, we'll fly through the night
When I close my eyes from this last glance
Come on pretty little thing
What harm could you cause me?
If only in our dreams are we free,
Dream with me moth and chance

Snow in July

Maybe I'll worry when the rain falls up from underneath me and
Maybe I'll worry when the world stops spinning and the seasons cease.
Maybe I'll worry when the wind won't blow and the sea won't come and go.
Maybe I'll worry when the sun won't shine and the stars won't glow...

But you and I both know that's as likely as Snow in July.
You and I both know that's as likely as Snow in July!

And maybe this could be why I appear not to care
When my whole world turns inside out upside down.
Well that will be the day when the pigs all fly away
And the birds all become grounded for a day,
When I'm dressed up in fame.
When I've won life's silly games.

But you and I both know that's as likely as Snow in July.
You and I both know that's as likely as Snow in July!

Solitary slumber

I wish you would come home.

I wish I could lie down and stop breathing safe in the knowledge you would fly home and rescue me.

I wish I were stiff and cold just so you would come and give me warmth.

To be positive you were coming home so we could go to bed together would be bliss

To never wake up alone would be heaven

But we are not gods. We do not live in heaven

And I do wake up alone

And when I return to solitary slumber again not knowing where you are, thinking you will be there when I wake up and you don't come back...

I'd rather not wake up at all.

Sunny morning

Warmth surrounds me. My calm heart beats gently against my chest and pulls me from my slumber. Oh the joys of Spring. That satisfaction of waking feeling refreshed and excited for the day. Children giggling in my arms, I skip down the stairs and the air becomes infused with sweet smells of cinnamon and freshly baked cakes.

It waits for me outside the window. I can feel its heat radiating as it frantically searches for tiny cracks in the curtains. Dust dances on laser-beams that form flecks on the floor where it peeps through. I take a breath. I let it in.

Whoosh! A river of light torrents past me, seeking out and saturating every dark corner. Incense smoke twists on the current and cascades out the door. Consumed in a total rush of elation as it engulfs me, it permeates my soul. It wraps its great, comforting arms around me and holds me tightly for a minute. I cannot move. Trapped in this euphoric embrace, my consciousness of time becomes warped and my care for life's petty problems diminishes. For this hazy moment, there is no money, no work, no bills. All I am aware of is the beautiful vibrance that is this moment. This is what I live for. I slump in a dopey heap on the sofa and bask in the rays that blast down on me and kiss my skin, leaving it prickly with ecstasy. Unfortunately, my idyllic escape is short lived.

A loud crash and a shrill squeal of achievement rings from the kitchen that promptly pulls me from my vegetative state. I apprehensively peer around the corner only to find my two-year-old son proudly displaying the freshly upturned dustbin and its contents on the floor. My nine-month-old daughter contentedly sat at his feet chewing on a black banana skin that she has already snatched from the pile.

Ah, it begins…

Sweet Neat Vodka

Where does the day go?
Nobody knows.
Don't step on my toes
Because I'm dancing to my own beat.

Where does the day go?
I couldn't say.
I drink it away
Sat by my window.

Where does the day go?
I couldn't tell.
Because I can't taste or smell
This alcohol anymore

And if I ask, will you come
And drown your sorrows with me
Drinking my sweet, neat vodka?

I tried to like you,
Tried to be nice,
Like sugar and spice
But I put a bad taste in your mouth.

Tried not to love you
But try as I may
It's my time I waste
I like your ego

But I hate the things you do

And the way you act
But still something attracts
My mind, body, soul

So If I ask, will you come?
And drown your sorrows with me
Drinking my sweet, neat vodka.

There'll come a day

There'll come a day
When you realise
And you feel the pain
You saw in my eyes
When you fall in love
Like you've never felt
And it gets hot
You see it starts to melt
Then you watch it burn
Down to the ground
And then you'll hear
That screaming sound
As it dies away
There'll come a day.

Terrible Twos

Who is this monster?
My sweet little lamb
Has grown tiny red horns and a long pointed tail
He chuckles
He is still so innocent even if he is guilty

I could scream at him
Sometimes I think I could smack him so hard it would bruise
Then what would they say?
Bad parent.
The reason wouldn't matter.
Child beater. Unsuitable mother.
Would it matter?
No.
I bite my tongue and send him to his step.

The relief of not reacting slightly settles my frustrated mind
Such anger in one second, pure guilt in the next
As his sorry little face sheepishly peers up at me through that curling
nest of beautiful blond hair.
The shame in his eyes as he holds my scornful gaze
And wipes a great green slug from his slimy nose with the grubby
cuff of his jumper.
How can I be angry with that?
Oh the emotional confusion that is parenthood!
It's like puppy training but never-ending,
Complete with puddles on the floor and torn wallpaper.

Still,
Even if the kitchen is flooded with milk

And all I see and hear are lights being flicked on and off and on and
off.
Even if the tumble dryer is now smoking and there is cutlery in the
microwave,
The oven is baking nothing and the hobs are burning tea towels,
Yes, even when all he does is cause chaos around me
This little terror is still my beloved perfect angel.

Trying to remember

Trying to remember
Something I forget
Is trying to begin
When I haven't got there yet.
It's attempting to listen to a song that isn't sung,
Trying to evaluate a work that's not begun.

Trying to remember
Something I forget
Is eating me alive
And burning a hole in my head
Remembering to remember but forgetting what it was
Failing to recall the simplest thing is hard because

Of all the things that I could relay
From my memory
At this very point in time
Are of no use to me.
Sine rule, algorithms, the first boy that I kissed;
Are not about to tell me what was on my shopping list.

Waltz With Me

Waltz with me! Waltz with me!
Through life's little fantasy
Open your eyes and find dream is reality.
Dance with me! Prance with me!
Float down the high street,
Swallow your nonsense and let it take hold…

Unexplainable emotions,
Unexplainable feeling inside,
All of this action mixed with this energy
Amounts to a force that's impossible to hide!
Swirling, spinning out of control
Open your mind up and let it unfold.
Notice a carnival of lights on the road
Come on, lets venture into the unknown…

And waltz with me! Waltz with me!
Through life's little fantasy
Open your eyes and find dream is reality
Dance with me! Prance with me!
Float down the high street,
Swallow your nonsense and let it take hold…

And rise with its downfall,
Flow up the waterfall.
Walk a strait line and you've done a full circle!
There's no time to stall,
Follow laughter, my inviting call…
Isn't this grand? Take my hand
And!

Waltz with me! Waltz with me!
Through life's little fantasy
Discover colours that no one has ever seen
Dance with me! Prance with me!
Float down the high street.
The stars are our spotlights,
The world is our ballroom…

Pitter patter

Pitter patter on the window ledge,
pitter patter in the street,
pitter patter ringing in my head,
pitter patter when I eat,
pitter patter when I go to bed,
and its never leaving me!
Just this pitter patter, pitter patter,
pitter patter, pitter patter
pitter patter, pitter patter
pitter patter,
mice.

You'll be with me

Don't weep for me, my mother dear
My soul is strong and free,
Just pluck a poppy from the earth
That way, you'll be with me.

Don't wish that I were with you
It never was to be
Just kiss that blood red poppy
That way, you'll be with me.

You must believe the stories
The terror I did see
Just hold that poppy to your heart
That way, you'll be with me.

The filth, the blood, the pestilence
The death, the agony
Feel pride towards that poppy
That way, you'll be with me.

Our deaths were not in vain, my love
Through us you too are free,
So dance among the poppies
That way, you'll be with me.